Hope for the Broken Girl

Hope Series
Book 3

by Crissi Langwell

"*The wound is the place where the Light enters you.*"

~ Rumi

Chapters

Broken

The engine whines as I turn the key, but refuses to turn over. I pull the keys out and throw them across the dash in frustration. The noise is louder than I expect and I glance in the back seat to see if Hope is still sleeping. She is.

With my phone in hand, I get out of the car, walking over to the passenger side so that I'm not next to the busy highway. The ocean spreads out in front of me in both directions, seeming to take up my whole world. I look down at the phone screen. My sleeves have hiked up my arms, and I pull them down out of habit to hide the bruises.

I don't know if he'll answer. He has no reason to answer. I'm afraid he'll ignore my call. Worse, I'm afraid he'll answer and give me hell for the way I disappeared. But I had no choice, just like I have no choice now.

His name isn't on my phone. I'm not that dumb. But I know his number by heart. I touch each digit, pausing with a deep breath before I hit the final one. Then I hold the phone to my ear and wait. He might not answer. He might not pick up the phone because he doesn't recognize this number. He might...

"Hello?"

I say nothing for a moment, closing my eyes at the sound of his voice. I hadn't realized how much it would affect me.

"Hello? Anyone there?"

"Jace." I keep my eyes closed, listening to him breathe in my ear as the coastal wind whips my hair around my face.

"Maddie?"

"Yes, it's me. I'm sorry it's so early."

"Oh my God, how are you? Where are you? Is everything okay?"

"No," I whisper.

"I can't hear you. There's a lot of noise on your end. Are you all right?"

I open my eyes and look out at the ocean. It's funny how something so large and dangerous can look beautiful and inviting from far away. Right now, it appears like glass under the first rays of the morning sun, despite the wind. It's deceptive—how could something so monstrous appear this peaceful?

"I need you to find me. I need you to bring me home," I tell him. He says nothing for a moment, and my doubts flare up, once again. *Please don't let me down.*

"Where are you?" he asks.

"I'm not sure. Hold on." I pull up a map on the phone. "I've just passed Crescent City." I glance down the highway. Cars whip by on the narrow road, and there doesn't seem to be anything close. "I'm out of gas and can't go any further."

He's quiet, and I know he's looking up my location.

"Crescent City is more than five hours north from here," he says.

"I know." I clench my hand against my jeans, praying he'll come get me. If he refuses, I don't know what I'll do.

"Are you on Highway 101?" he asks.

"Yes," I say, sighing. It's way out of the way. I should have driven down I-5, but a detour at Grants Pass got me confused. I know I'd be closer to home if I hadn't gotten turned around. Now, I'm still too close to the Oregon border...too close to danger.

"Okay. There's a motel called Seaport Inn along the highway. Can you find it and tell me how far you are from it?"

I pull the phone from my ear and punch the name in.

"About three miles," I tell him.

"Can you walk that far?" he asks. I look in the back seat. Hope's still asleep in her car seat. I'll have to leave it behind, along with anything else that's too heavy to carry with Hope on my hip.

"I'm going to have to," I tell him. "But bring Kayci's car seat."

He tells me he'll call the motel and reserve a room with two beds, and to just show up and give them my name.

"I'll be there as soon as I can," he assures me. He's quiet for a moment, but I hear him breathing. "Will you be okay?" he finally asks. "Are you in any kind of trouble? Is there anything I should know to prepare myself?"

I don't know how to answer. I look up to the sky. The cloudless blue is deceiving. The wind stills for a moment, and my breath comes out in small clouds. I pull my jacket closer to my body.

"No," I lie. "Just hurry."

After we hang up, I stare at my phone a few minutes, dreading the three-mile hike down the highway. I'll have cars rushing past on one side, and a sheer drop to the ocean on the other—all while holding a toddler who'll probably get tired of being carried.

The location services arrow is still visible at the top of my phone screen. I shut out of the maps running in the background, and I shiver when the arrow stays. Opening the settings app, I scroll through the different programs to see which is monitoring my location. Find My iPhone. He's found me. I open the app and check to see where Jordan is. He's still in Oregon, but his icon is moving down the highway.

"He must have borrowed Cody's car," I whisper. If I stay where I am, he'll find me in three hours—at least two hours before Jace gets here.

I log out of the app and try to delete it. I'm frustrated that it won't delete, remaining as one of the core apps on my overpriced phone. I turn off my location services altogether. Even that doesn't calm my nerves. I hold the phone for a moment, contemplating my next move. Then I wind my arm back and throw the phone as hard as I can into the ocean. It takes forever to fall, disappearing in the waves directly below me. I regret throwing it as soon as it's gone. If anything happens, I have no way to seek help. But I can't take any chances. If Jordan finds me, it's all over.

After seeing Jordan's moving icon, a three-hour window doesn't seem very long. I open the passenger side door and lift my backpack off the floorboard. Inside is all I have left of the life I've been living for six months—a change of clothes for Hope and me, our toothbrushes, my wallet and ID, plus a few snacks. I don't have any money—it all belongs to Jordan.

Hope stirs when I open the back door, grimacing when I start to unbuckle her. She opens her eyes as I put her jacket over her arms.

"Where's Daddy?" she asks, looking around.

"He's at home, sweetie." She scowls, but doesn't cry or ask any more questions. I'm glad she doesn't know any better. I don't think I could explain this to her if I tried. I'm ashamed of everything she's witnessed.

She rests her head on my shoulder as we make our way down the side of the road. I'm grateful for this; there's no way I'd let her walk on this busy highway. The cars are careful to move around us, but my heart lurches every time we reach a blind corner. At least it's daylight.

I shift Hope from one side to the other every time she gets heavy. The third time I do this, I'm startled when a truck pulls onto the side of the road and parks in front of me. There's a man in the driver's seat, and no one next to him. I stop; afraid it's Jordan. But I see his hair is longer and he's wearing a hat, unlike Jordan's sculpted short hair. Still, his presence makes me nervous. I have no choice but to walk past the truck. I pull the hood of my jacket over my head, and keep my eyes to the ground as I move forward.

"Hey," the driver says as I start to walk by. I ignore him and walk faster. "Hey!" he calls. I stop and turn, my hands sweating under Hope's legs as I keep looking down. "It's pretty dangerous to be walking along this stretch of road. Where you headed? Can I give you girls a lift?"

I shake my head no, and start to turn around.

"Look, I'm not dangerous, and I won't try anything, I promise. But I'd never forgive myself if I drove away and something happened to you. Let me at least drive you into town."

I think over his offer. I probably have two more miles to go. I'm cold and hungry. My arms ache from holding Hope. Plus, I'm afraid Jordan will drive by at any moment, even though he's still hundreds of miles away. I nod, and walk over to the passenger side of the truck. Refusing to look at him, I open the door and get in. I keep Hope in my lap, and put the backpack at my feet.

"I don't have a car seat, but I'll drive slow so your little girl will be safe," the man says. "I'm Christian." He holds his hand out to shake mine, but I keep my hands wrapped around Hope.

"You can drop me off at the Seaport Inn," I mumble. He moves his hand away, clearing his throat.

"You got it, little lady," he says. He puts his blinker on and waits for a break in traffic. Then he pulls onto the road. We drive in silence the rest of the way to the motel. I stare out the window, angry as a few tears escape despite my efforts to not cry. I'm almost safe.

"Here you are." Christian pulls up in front of the motel. I open the door, clutching Hope as I hop out. I turn for my backpack, and then look at the driver. His smile fades. I pull my hood forward again, averting my eyes. "Are you okay?" he asks. "Do I need to call someone?"

I shake my head. I start to leave, but he reaches for my hand. Out of instinct, I jerk away.

"I'm serious," he says. "Do you need help?"

I shake my head again, but this time I look up into his concerned eyes.

"Everything's going to be okay now," I tell him. He nods. Then he opens his glove box, taking out an old receipt and pen. He scribbles something on the paper, then hands it to me.

"Just in case," he says. I look down to see his name and phone number.

"Thanks." I close the door and walk toward the motel. I throw the paper in the garbage before I step into the lobby. Luckily, the girl at the front desk has no customer service skills; she doesn't look up from her computer as she searches for Jace's name and asks for my ID.

With the key card in hand, I leave the lobby and search for the room number printed on the card holder. Once I find it, I let myself in, closing the door behind me and locking it.

Only then can I relax.

I turn the TV on for Hope, using it as an electronic babysitter while I go to the bathroom. My bladder is near bursting, and I sigh at the sudden release of pressure. I wash my hands, staring at the girl looking back at me, taking in the deep purple around her eye, and the way her nose now has a slight lean to it. I gently touch the gash on my cheek, wincing at the sting.

"He really did a number on you this time, didn't he?" I whisper to my reflection. I feel stupid. Why did I stay for so long? There are so many *should haves* in my mind. The first moment of violence *should have* been the last. I *should have* stayed in Petaluma. I *should have* left before he got meaner. I *should have* thought about the example I was setting for my daughter.

I thought I loved him. Then I thought I deserved this. I thought a lot of things, and now I don't know what to believe. I don't even know if I'm safe, holed up in some random motel, waiting for Jace to rescue me. I know I'll never be free from danger. Jordan can still find me; he can still do everything he swore he'd do if I ever left him. I might have caused even more trouble just by leaving. But I couldn't stay.

Now, all I can do is wait.

Six months earlier

Free

I looked down at the bruise on my wrist. For a moment, I forgot where it came from. Then I remembered the way Jordan squeezed my wrist when I tried to get my phone from him. *He was just mad. It wasn't like he was trying to hurt me.* He was usually so gentle. It was a mistake.

"What are you thinking about?" Jordan asked. I pulled my sweatshirt over my wrist. I wasn't sure why, but I didn't want him to see the bruise. It embarrassed me. I hoped it would fade soon.

"Nothing," I told him. "I'm just nervous, and excited." It was true, I *was* excited. But I was also worried. My last words to Charlie had been hateful. It had been so close to Viola's death, and I'd yelled at him for meddling as if he were my father. I told him he wasn't my dad, yet he was the closest thing I had to a dad in my life. For the past two years, he'd made sure Hope and I had a roof over our heads, food in our bellies, and every comfort we needed to set us up for a secure life. But then I took off in the middle of the night with Jordan. I kept trying to push my guilt away, but I was drowning.

Jordan reached over and squeezed my leg. Despite my hurting heart, I smiled, my insides fluttering at his touch.

"There's nothing to be worried about," he said, rubbing my thigh. "I'm taking care of you and Hope now. We're finally a family. This is how it's supposed to be."

"I know, but I feel bad that I never said goodbye to Charlie."

I regretted the words as soon as they left my mouth. Jordan's jaw clenched, and he removed his hand from my thigh and put it back on the steering wheel. "Jordan." I touched his arm. He didn't move away, and I took that as a good sign. "It's just that he did so much for Hope and me. He and Viola took us in; they took care of us. Without them, I never could have raised Hope."

"Because you tried to give her away," he said. I took my hand away from his arm as he said it, scooting away from him, angrily staring out the window.

"I thought you understood. I told you. I didn't know what to do. I was homeless and you weren't around. I couldn't let her live on the streets. I tried to give her up because I loved her, not because I didn't want her."

I focused on the scenery whipping by, even when I heard him sigh.

"I didn't mean anything by it." I wanted to believe him, but wasn't sure he'd ever understand what I'd gone through. "Look, I owe it to Charlie for stepping in when I wasn't able to. But I'm here now, and he'd only stand in our way if you went on living there. I mean, it's best if we're all together again, right? Charlie made it seem like I didn't belong."

"I know," I murmured. I faced the front, kicking my feet up on the dash. "He loves us, and is very protective. He doesn't know you like I do."

"Fine, but can you really tell me he'd take the time to *get* to know me? All he did was judge me. I tried to dress nice to impress him. I was polite to him, and I listened to everything he said. I even pretended to like sports because he seemed interested, but all he saw was a guy with ink who works in a tattoo shop. It didn't matter what I said to him, he'd never believe I was good enough for you."

I knew he was telling the truth. It was the only reason I agreed to pack a bag of clothes, wake Hope, and steal away in the middle of the night. Plus, I knew Jordan and I were meant to raise Hope together.

I turned and looked at our sleeping daughter, noticing the rays from the rising sun hitting her little face. I adjusted the sunshade next to her so she wouldn't burn. She had no idea what was going on, and I wondered how she'd react when she woke up. Would she miss Charlie? Would she ask for Fátima? Or would she accept their absence, like she'd accepted Viola's death? I worried about her reaction, but knew this was for the best. If Hope had the chance to be raised and loved by both of her parents, I wasn't about to take that away.

We stopped at a gas station close to the Oregon border. While Jordan filled the tank, I got out to stretch my legs.

"You know we have to get rid of this car, right?" Jordan asked. I paused, unsure if I heard him correctly.

"What? No," I said. The white Honda had been a graduation gift from Charlie. It was the first big thing I'd ever owned, and the last thing he gave me. It was like keeping part of him with me.

"All he has to do is report this car stolen, and I go to jail."

"But you didn't steal it," I said. "It's my car."

"Technically it's Charlie's car. Your name isn't on the registration." He nodded toward the glove box. "If you don't believe me, go check."

I opened the latch. The registration was on top, and Charlie's name stared out at me. The insurance underneath had my name on it, though. I leaned out of the car and waved the papers at him.

"The insurance is in my name. That's some proof that we're allowed to have the car, right?" Even I knew my argument was weak.

"If Charlie calls to report his car missing, the cops will be on the lookout. He may have already called it in. If they catch us, and he decides to press charges—and he will—I go to jail, you go back to him, and we never see each other again. He'll make sure of it—that's a promise."

"Charlie wouldn't do that," I insisted.

"Really? You don't think he'd use this as the perfect opportunity to get me out of your life for good? Because that would be the way to do it."

He was right. At this moment, Charlie was probably wondering where I was. By the end of the day, he'd have every cop in the county searching for me. Still, I couldn't bear to give up the last piece of my life in Petaluma.

"Isn't there another way?" He wrinkled his brow in thought, then looked at me and shrugged.

"I suppose we could switch the license plate or something, and paint it a different color once we get to my buddy's place in Oregon."

I nodded at this, smiling in relief. It wasn't a perfect solution, but it allowed me to keep the car.

I heard Hope stirring behind me and turned in my seat. "Hey, pretty girl. You want to get out and go potty?" She frowned and shook her head. "Well, let's get out anyway and try. Okay, baby?"

"No, Mama!" she said as I unbuckled the seat belt. I ignored her protests. If we didn't go now, she'd wet her car seat.

"I'll be right back," I said. Jordan reached into his pocket and handed me a $10.

"Get us a couple hot dogs while you're in there, okay? I'm starving."

I took the money and carried Hope to the gas station's mini-mart. She continued arguing with me, but emptied her bladder as I balanced her over the large toilet.

"There, that wasn't so bad, now was it?" I told her not to touch anything in the dirty stall while I took my turn. Then we washed up and headed toward the cash register. I bought a few hot dogs and a soda to split, then went outside. The car wasn't next to the pump, and I looked around until I saw Jordan parked off to the side of the lot. He was leaning against the car, smoking. He put it out as we came closer, and took the hot dog I held out to him. I was still unwrapping mine as he finished his in two bites.

"Well, that should tide me over for the next half hour."

"There's more inside if you're still hungry." I tore a few pieces off the hot dog and gave them to Hope before taking a bite. As soon as the juices hit my taste buds, I realized what he meant. It was just an overcooked gas station hot dog, but it made me realize how hungry I was. "Maybe we should each get another one."

"Do you mind?" he asked. "Is there any change?" I nodded, patting the few dollars and coins in my pocket.

"Watch Hope," I said, handing him the rest of my hot dog. "And make sure you give her small pieces so she doesn't choke."

I went back inside and bought two more hot dogs. When I returned, my heart expanded when I saw Jordan walking slowly, holding Hope's hand. She still didn't know him well, and didn't understand what having a father meant. Just a few weeks ago, she didn't even know he existed. What was I supposed to tell her? That I gave birth to her in the middle of a vineyard and tried to give her away, my home had been a pile of clothes behind a grocery store, and I'd been arrested for stealing some woman's wallet while her dad took off? Did I tell her he'd been in jail her whole first year, and missed everything?

Of course not.

She was too little to understand. But I had a hard time knowing what I'd tell her when she *was* old enough. Could I explain why I made the choices I did? I didn't know. All I knew was what was in front of me, and that was Jordan being a daddy to our little girl. Seeing them together made me sure of my decision. We were supposed to be together, and I wasn't going to let anything get in our way. If the car had to be stripped of paint, I'd let it happen. Hell, if we ended up having to trade it in, I wouldn't argue. I was willing to forget everyone I left back home if it allowed us to be a family.

As soon as I thought this, Jace came to mind. His last text was still in my broken phone, now scattered in pieces in Charlie's driveway. I knew I'd never talk with him again. I'd made my choice; I was moving forward. Still, I felt sad knowing I'd never see him again. Or Charlie. Or Fátima….

"Stop it," I whispered. I waved at Jordan as he scooped Hope into his arms. She squealed as he tossed her up and caught her.

"Careful!" I said as I reached them and handed Jordan his hot dog.

"Mama, more!" Hope said, pushing against Jordan in an effort to get to me and my hot dog.

"Here, baby," Jordan said, breaking off a piece of his hot dog. She opened her mouth and he put it inside.

A family. This is the way it's supposed to be. There's no time for regrets.

Back on the road, I asked where we were going. Jordan said we were headed for Eugene. He told me about his friend, Cody, and the farm he lived on. Every year, they hired workers from all over to help with the fall harvest because it was such a big job. I couldn't miss how perfect this was for me. Working in Charlie's vineyards and tending to Viola's garden gave me many of the skills I'd need to work on a farm. When Jordan told me about the house we'd live in on the farm, I got even more excited. This was the right kind of place to raise Hope. Maybe she'd grow up wanting to work with plants, too.

When we reached the Oregon border, our surroundings changed quickly. California was yellow and dry from years of drought, but Oregon was lush and green. We headed through a forest of towering redwoods, and I opened my window to inhale the fresh scent. Along with the clean air, I caught a whiff of marijuana. I turned to Jordan.

"Nothing like that green air, right?" he said before I could say anything. "It's legal here, so everyone's growing it."

"*Everyone?*"

"Well, not everyone. You still have to have permits to grow large quantities. But the opportunity to make a lot of money is here. Hell, I'd grow it if I could."

I grimaced, but said nothing. I knew Jordan had smoked a little back in New Mexico, and I was pretty sure he still did after we moved to San Francisco. But I'd never gathered the courage to try it. Now that I was a mom, I definitely didn't want to, and didn't want Hope around it, either.

"Are people just getting high in the forest or something?" I asked.

"No, those are the plants," he said. "They're probably hidden among the trees by people who don't have permits, though they're hardly a secret with that odor. I'm pretty sure the cops have just given up trying to sniff them all out."

After a stop for lunch, it took us about three more hours to reach the gates of where we'd be staying. Two men stood there, and I noticed their rifles. They carried them casually, but I could tell they were ready to reach for them if necessary by the way their hands hovered near the grip. I was relieved they didn't see us as a threat as they approached our car. One came close to us while the other seemed to stand guard behind him.

"Hey, what's up?" The way he said it, it was clear this wasn't a friendly question.

"I'm here to see Cody," Jordan said. "He's expecting us."

He peered into the car, looking at Hope in the back seat, and then at me. Something in his expression made me feel uneasy. I put my hand in Jordan's, but he brushed me away.

The guy turned back to Jordan. "What's your name?"

"Jordan Turner. This is my girlfriend, Maddie Russo, and our daughter, Hope. We'll be staying here. Cody has a place set up for us."

"Ah, so you're the prince," the guy said with a sarcastic laugh. "Not everyone gets their own cabin. Cody must really like you." He nodded at the guy behind him, who moved to open the gate. Jordan touched his finger to his forehead as a kind of salute, and we drove on through.

"I have a feeling that guy will give me trouble," he said. I didn't have time to ask why because as we pulled up, a muscular man came out of a warehouse-style building and over to greet us. Jordan put the car in park and turned off the ignition.

"Cody," he said, getting out of the car. They clapped each other on the back as if they'd been friends for years. I was reminded again how little I knew about my boyfriend. I suddenly felt shy and awkward. Jordan was walking into this new life of ours with people he already knew. I knew no one.

"Who's this?" Cody nodded at me in the car.

"This is my girl, Maddie," Jordan said. "And in the back seat is our daughter, Hope."

"Oh shit, man, I didn't know you were a dad," Cody said. He reached over and shook my hand. "Nice to meet you, Maddie."

"Nice to meet you, too." I smelled the marijuana in the air, and Cody's eyes were half closed. What had Jordan signed us up for?

"Let me show you your digs," Cody said. I got Hope out of the back seat and we followed Cody to our new house. To call it a house was generous. It reminded me of one of the bungalows at my high school. I took in the peeling white paint, a cracked window, and a ramp leading to the front door. The linoleum-floored rooms smelled musty. The house trapped the summer heat, and I had a feeling the winters would be freezing. A portable heater in one corner showed I was right. This place would be miserable when the cold weather came.

Cody gave us the grand tour, which took all of two minutes. The living room had an old futon covered with a sheet. To the right was a small kitchen with an electric stove and a sink with a dripping faucet. One cupboard door was missing from the hinges, leaning against the wall near the sink instead.

There was only one bathroom, but I was glad to see the shower also had a tub, even if it needed a good scrubbing. If I had to live in this dump, I at least wanted a place where I could soak at the end of the day. Also, I couldn't imagine bathing Hope in a shower.

The bedroom, the one with the cracked window, had a bed and a dresser. When Jordan saw me eyeing the window, he promised he'd fix it right away. I was sure Duct tape was part of his fix-it plan.

"That's all of it," Cody said. "You guys are lucky. Most of the workers just bunk in the warehouse. But when Jordan said he was bringing you, Maddie, I couldn't just give you guys a bunk bed. I had to set you up in the penthouse. Glad I did, now that I know you've got a kid."

"I didn't know how to tell you," Jordan said. "I wasn't sure how you felt about having kids here."

"Hey man, it's all good. It's a first, but it'll work out. Besides, you're my boy." He turned to me. "This guy here is like a brother to me. We were locked up together, and he always had my back. I told him if he ever needed a job, he had one here with me." He looked back at Jordan. "I'm just glad you took me up on it. It will be like old times."

"Better than old times," Jordan said. "Here, we're free."

"Well, freer than behind bars, at least," Cody said. "Make no mistake, we're never truly free."

3

Ours

After Cody left, Jordan got our things out of the car while I looked for cleaning supplies. I was relieved to find a bottle of cleaning spray and paper towels under the kitchen sink. I winced when I set Hope on the couch, trying not to imagine the mites and cockroaches that might be hiding in the folded-up foam mattress, and told her to stay there while I sprayed everything down.

"Jeez, Maddie, it's not like the plague is in this house," Jordan said, setting our bags on the floor.

"Put them over there," I said, pointing to a corner. "I haven't cleaned that spot yet. And I'm not cleaning out plague, I'm just being careful. We don't know who lived here before us, or what was on these surfaces. If they did any kind of drugs, or if anyone..." I shuddered as I thought of some of the horrible things that could have happened in our new home. "I don't want Hope to accidentally touch anything dangerous or gross."

"Fair enough. Better you than me. I hate cleaning."

I had a flashback to the last conversation we'd had with Charlie, the one before Jordan blew up and left the house.

"Tonight, you came over here for a meal with our family," Charlie had said. *"I watched as Maddie made sure Hope was fed, bathed, and put to bed. Then she cleaned the kitchen, and tended to Hope once more. You didn't offer to help her, not once. You made me your priority when you should have made Maddie and Hope your priority. So when you say you're going to split all the responsibilities of raising a family down the middle, I don't believe you. After all, you took off three years ago and let her be responsible for raising your child on her own. What's going to stop you from leaving now?"*

Jordan went back outside for more of our stuff, and I watched him from the window. He stopped to talk with Cody, who introduced him to other workers. Jordan shook their hands, then went back to the car and loaded up with the rest of our belongings. Arms full, he gave me a grin as our eyes met through the window.

"You're wrong, Charlie," I whispered. So Jordan hated cleaning. I hated cleaning, too. But we all have to do things we don't like. I was glad to have Jordan unloading the car. We were working as a team. Sometimes that meant one of us picked up the slack. But the other could do the same in different circumstances. It would all even out in the end.

It didn't take long to unpack everything and put it away. There wasn't much to begin with. I regretted not bringing more. There was one old pan and a pot in the kitchen, but no plates or forks. There were sheets on the bed, but I would rather have died than sleep on them. There were no towels, and the only roll of toilet paper was half-gone. We also had no food except a few snacks we'd bought at the last pit stop.

"You stay here with Hope, and I'll get what we need from the store," Jordan said. I shook my head.

"I want to go with you." I didn't want to stay cooped up in this house, surrounded by people I didn't know.

"It'll take longer if we all go," Jordan said. "I'm hungry, and I don't want to wait to get something to eat."

"We could go out to eat first, then go shopping."

"Maddie, please," he said. "Let me just get what we need. I won't be gone more than an hour."

"What am I supposed to do while you're gone? I don't know anyone; there's nothing for Hope to do here. We'll be bored out of our minds."

He kissed me on the cheek and grabbed the keys to the car. "You'll figure something out, I'm sure." He left, and all I could do was watch. I heard him call out to Cody over by the warehouse, who trotted over to the car. They chatted a moment, then Cody called out to a group of guys before getting into the passenger seat of my car. I fumed as they drove away. Now I had to figure out what to do until he got back.

The house felt humid, and I tried to open the windows. None of them would budge. Afraid to break another window like the one in the bedroom, I let it be. I wanted to open a door or something, but didn't want to risk Hope running outside. Truthfully, though, it was more about keeping everyone else out. With the doors closed, I didn't have to face any of the strangers on this farm.

Hope was playing with a few rocks on the floor. I'd gathered them while we were unpacking and cleaning the house, and had shown her how to put them in the cooking pot. This had kept her attention the whole time. She liked the clanging sound every time she dropped in a rock or dumped them out.

"Who needs toys when you have rocks?" I said, amused at the cheap entertainment. I got down on the floor, and we made a game out of the rocks. After a while, though, this got old. While she was still enjoyed the toy idea, I knew it wouldn't last long. I wished I'd planned better when I packed our bags. I could have gathered toys, books, or other things to occupy her time. All we had were the walls around us, and a hard floor. I felt stir crazy, and realized I couldn't stay cooped up forever. There was no telling when Jordan would be back, and the house was getting stuffier by the minute. "What do you say we go for a walk?" I asked, picking up the pot of rocks and putting it on the counter.

"Mine!" I scooped her up, ignoring her complaints.

"We're going outside." She pushed against me, but stopped when I grabbed the bag of chips of the counter. I gave her one, and then we left the house for the fresh air outside.

I stayed away from the warehouse, unwilling to be near the guys outside. I'd wait for Jordan to come back before getting introductions. Instead, Hope and I explored the wooded area behind our bungalow. There were a few more shabby cottages scattered among the trees, and a few tents set up. I carried Hope beyond the tents until we were deep in the woods, away from everyone. We found a creek—a perfect diversion while we waited for Jordan. We tossed rocks into the water and dug for interesting things in the dirt. Hope giggled as two fat squirrels raced up a tree and jumped from one branch to another, playing chase. Sitting near the creek, surrounded by singing birds and gurgling water, I found comfort in this strange place. I missed home, and felt sad and guilty every time I thought about how I left Charlie. But this small oasis brought me peace.

The sun was setting fast, and dark shadows spread through the forest. I picked up Hope and we made our way back to the farm. I wished I'd marked the trail as I searched for anything familiar. Everything looked the same. Every tree was identical. Every stone, every pine needle... I tried not to panic, determined to find our way through the woods. Finally, I spotted one of the tents, and I followed the nearby trail until the warehouse came in view. I saw my car, which meant Jordan was back. I walked up the ramp and into the house.

"Jordan?"

No one answered, but bags filled with groceries sat on the counter and floor. He'd bought a new sheet set, towels and washcloths, soap and shampoo, even a few toys. I let Hope play with the toys as I unpacked. I stripped the stained sheets from the bed, replacing them with crisp new ones, then added the blankets we'd brought from Petaluma. Now it looked like a real bed.

I kept looking out the window, wondering when Jordan was coming back. I scrubbed the pans with a new sponge. Then I cooked chicken, rice, and frozen vegetables. I searched the bags for salt, but found none. It'd be bland, but would still be home-cooked.

Without a table, Hope and I sat on the floor, eating off paper plates. Some of her food spilled, and I was glad I'd disinfected the linoleum as she picked up the dropped pieces and put them in her mouth. I left the rest in the pot for whenever Jordan came back.

"I done!" Hope exclaimed, pulling her plate up and putting it on her head. The rest of her food landed in her hair before I could stop her.

"Well, that's one way to finish your food," I sighed. She made a funny face, and I had to laugh. I took the last few bites of my food, then threw our plates into one of the empty garbage bags. "How about a bath?" I asked. She looked down at her shirt covered with bits of rice, then tried to take it off.

"Help, Mama."

I carried her in the bathroom and stripped off her clothes. She played in the water until it was time to wash her hair. Jordan had bought adult shampoo, not the tear-free baby kind. I massaged a small amount of shampoo into her scalp without getting any in her eyes, but knew rinsing would be a challenge. Sure enough, she fought me as I leaned her back and poured water from a cup onto her hair. She screamed as some got in her eyes.

"You have to stay still, baby." She cried, rubbing her eyes, which only got more soap in them. I wet a washcloth, then swiped the soap from her face. "Hold this over your eyes and they won't get soapy." She did, and I got the rest of the shampoo out of her hair without any more tears. When done, I wrapped her in a clean towel and took her into my room to put on new pajamas.

"Where's your daddy?" I asked, ruffling her hair with the towel. She giggled at the motion, while I fought my loneliness and anger that Jordan still hadn't come home. It was our first night as a family. I thought he'd be here with us. I thought this would mean more to him.

Hope reached for me and I scooped her up and took her into the living room so I could make her bed. I hadn't unfolded the futon and dreaded what I would find, but the mattress seemed fine when I laid it flat. I sprayed it with disinfectant, then covered it with one of the fitted sheets Jordan bought. It was too big, but I tucked the edges around the corners. Then I sat down and Hope climbed up next to me.

"Ready to sleep in your big girl bed?" In Petaluma, I'd been preparing myself for the day she'd be out of her crib, but I hadn't been ready yet. Even though she knew how to climb over the top, I couldn't bring myself to get her a toddler bed. Now, I had no choice. I wasn't sure she'd even stay in it, now that she had the freedom to roam around the house. This would be interesting.

"You sleep too, Mama," Hope said, putting her head down and reaching for me. I covered her with a blanket, then laid down next to her. I had a few hours until my own bedtime, but lying down felt good. I hadn't realized how tired I was, plus I wasn't sure what to do after Hope went to bed. I had no TV, no books, no journal…nothing. All I'd be able to do was fidget and look out the window until Jordan finally came home.

"I'll be here for a little while." I listened to her breathe, waiting for her to fall asleep before I moved to the bedroom, feeling the anger burning into my chest at being left alone on our first night.

***

"Babe, wake up."

My body felt heavy and my eyes had a hard time opening. When I finally did, it took a few seconds to remember where we were. I rolled over to Jordan sitting on the edge of the futon.

"What time is it?" I whispered.

"Almost two." My anger returned, and I took a deep breath. I could smell the beer on him. "Sorry, we lost track of time."

"Were you drinking?" I asked him.

"A few beers, that's all. Come to bed."

I rolled over so that my back was facing him. "I'm afraid to leave Hope alone in here. She's never slept in a regular bed before."

"She'll be fine. She's asleep. Come to bed."

I wanted to argue with him. I wanted to know why he decided to hang out with a bunch of guys drinking beer, leaving us alone in the house. I wanted him to know how mad I was. But I didn't want to wake Hope. Without speaking, I got up and followed him to the bedroom. He undressed, then patted the mattress next to him. I got in bed, but kept my clothes on.

"What's wrong?"

"Seriously? What's wrong? Hope and I have been by ourselves almost since we got here, and you're asking what's wrong?"

"I said I was sorry."

"But you're not! You didn't even check on us! I don't know anyone here. I don't have anything to do. But you got to go drive wherever you wanted in *my* car, and then hang out with your buddies getting drunk."

"Hey, I got toys for Hope! I got food and everything else you need. I put gas in your car. I did all this with my own money, and you didn't even thank me."

"I'll give you money, if that's what you're asking for."

"That's not what I'm asking for. I'm asking for a little gratitude." He got up and stalked to the corner of the room. I could hear him unzipping his backpack. Then he tossed something on the bed. "I got you this, too."

I felt the box on the bed, and picked it up. I was still mad, but softened when I saw the familiar Apple logo.

"You got me an iPhone?"

"Yeah, but I don't do anything for you." He flopped onto the bed, and then rolled over to face the wall.

I stared at his back, struggling between anger and guilt.

"I just wasn't sure where you were or how to get hold of you. And…thank you."

"You're welcome."

The phone felt heavy in my hands. It was too much. I was glad to have it, but I hadn't even asked for it. Now he was mad at me. My resentment remained, expanding inside my chest—but it felt wrong to be angry.

"What were you doing all this time?"

"Working on your car." He kept his back to me. "We switched out the license plate and started sanding off the paint. I didn't know how long it would take."

Now I really felt like a jerk.

"I didn't know. I'm sorry," I told him. He rolled over to face me.

"Did you guys eat?" he asked. I nodded.

"I made a rice dish. I kept it in the pot on the stove for a while, but finally put it in the fridge so it wouldn't go bad. You can probably heat it up if you're still hungry."

"Nah, I got a burrito while I was out, and the guys had a bunch of snacks in the warehouse."

This pissed me off, but I was still holding the iPhone he gave me and there didn't seem to be much of a point in fighting.

"Why don't you put that fancy phone down and come here?"

The last thing I wanted to do was fool around. It had been a long day, and after sitting home alone all night, I wasn't feeling affectionate. But when he pulled me closer, my shoulders lowered and my reasons to push him away began to disappear. I'd been alone all day, and it felt good to be in his arms.

"You're wearing too many clothes," he whispered. "I can help you with that." He fumbled with my shirt, and I sucked in my breath as his fingers touched my skin. He was winning, but I wasn't ready to give in yet. I curled up to keep him from taking any of my clothes off, but he was stronger than I was. I rolled my eyes as he pulled my shirt over my head. I was too tired to argue, so I played along. Once undressed, he was inside of me. "You need a condom," I whispered.

"Come on, Maddie, we could start making brothers and sisters for Hope right away. We could have a dozen babies if you want." He started moving inside me. I caught my breath, unable to deny how good this felt.

"Not a dozen," I whispered against his ear as he continued to move. "And no babies now. Let's wait a while, make things more permanent. At least wait until we have our own place."

"Okay," he said, pushing harder. I clutched his back, pressing my face against his shoulder to keep from crying out.

"Condom," I whispered as soon as I caught my breath.

"I'll pull out," he whispered back.

"Promise?"

He said nothing as he continued to move. He grabbed my mouth with his, and I was suddenly lost in his kiss. I felt the tension growing inside me, and arched my back to allow him to have all of me. He met my invitation, and gripped my hips as he thrust forward. I felt my orgasm coming as he pulled out so he could finish. He collapsed on the bed, and I stared at the ceiling, more frustrated than ever.

"Well, it's not a perfect system, but it gets the job done, I guess," Jordan said.

"Yup," I said, gritting my teeth. I turned over to go to sleep, but he pulled me close and spooned me. He nestled his face against my neck, and I felt his lips touch my skin.

"I love you," he whispered. It was the first intimacy he'd shown all day, and I couldn't help it. I melted in his arms. But I also decided to buy condoms the next time I went to the store.

4

Torn

Cody showed us around the farm the next day. My job was to tend the crops near the warehouse, and help sell produce at the farmers' markets. Jordan, on the other hand, would be helping a crew in a plantation that required an ATV to get there.

"I don't get why we can't work in the same area of the farm," I whispered to Jordan when Cody was a few feet in front of us. As Hope played with my hair, I tried to work out how she'd fit into this new schedule of ours.

"It's because we have different skills," Jordan said.

"Do those skills have anything to do with that skunky smell I keep getting a whiff of?"

The same smell I'd noticed the day before was stronger in the morning, and I was starting to understand there was more to this farm than I could see. Jordan's guilty grin gave him away, and I stopped. I couldn't believe I'd been so stupid.

"Don't be like that," Jordan said.

"Is there a problem?" Cody asked, turning to see what the holdup was.

"Give us a few, okay man?" Jordan said. Cody nodded and headed for the warehouse.

"I never would have come here if I knew we were going to live on a pot farm."

"It's just a plant, only one of many grown here. And it's legal to grow here."

"Yeah, and I'm sure with the armed guys at the gate and the ATV drive to the marijuana plants, everything's legit, right?"

When Jordan didn't say anything, I started back toward the bungalow.

"Where are you going?"

"I'm leaving," I said. "I shouldn't have come with you in the first place. I had a home, and a life. Things were safe. It was a good place to raise Hope. This is not a good environment for our daughter. I never would have brought her here if I knew any of this."

"That's why I couldn't tell you," Jordan said. I stopped and spun around.

"So you got me to come with you based on a lie?"

"I never lied. I just didn't tell you everything. I was afraid you'd refuse to come, and I couldn't risk that. You and Hope are everything to me."

"Then why couldn't you plan for a life that's best for all of us?"

"That's what I'm doing!" Jordan insisted. "You think I want this kind of life for us? I don't. It's so we can make a life for ourselves and be a family. It's the fastest way to get money so we can go buy our own plot of land and a farm."

I closed my eyes and fought the temptation to give in. I hated that he knew me so well. *Of course* I wanted everything he said. I wanted us to be a family. I loved the idea of having our own farm. But I hated this whole life we'd signed on for. We were living in a shack on a pot farm. This was where we would be raising our daughter, for months, maybe years. I'd left a sure deal to live in a place like this.

"We could raise chickens and goats," he continued. "Have as many dogs as you want, and acres of vegetables you could sell from a booth at the farmers' market. Hope would learn how to garden, and we'd do this as a family. You'd get to stay home with her and raise our kids instead of putting them in daycare while you work a job you hate. This whole pot farm thing is temporary until we can afford our dream. I want to be with you, and this is the best way to get what we want."

"But, we could have done this with normal jobs," I said. "You could work at an auto dealership around here instead, or find a tattoo parlor or something. I can work nights waiting tables, or maybe watch a bunch of kids during the day. Or both!"

"And then put all our money toward rent and utilities? We'd never be able to save money that way. Here, we get to live rent-free, and our utilities are paid for. Our only expenses are food and gas, and any personal items we need. Other than that, the money we earn goes in our pockets. The pay will be incredible, and we can save a lot over a short amount of time. We may even have enough by the end of this year."

I looked up at the sky, taking a deep breath. This was so crazy. This was stupid. I looked back at him.

"So, six months, and we leave, right?" I said.

"I'm not promising that, Maddie. But I think it's possible."

"I don't think I can live here longer than that."

"So, you're saying yes, then?"

I sighed, shaking my head. But he knew, wrapping his arms around both Hope and me while he kissed my forehead.

"This isn't as bad as you think," he said. "You won't be around any of the pot. Taking care of the garden here will give you a taste of what it will be like when we have our own farm. You'll love it, I promise."

***

Things got busier over the next few weeks. Jordan was in the fields most days, and didn't come back until late. When he didn't work the fields, he spent afternoons sleeping and the nights in the warehouse, harvesting. He told me not to go near the warehouse; he was uneasy around the workers that kept coming in. I wasn't concerned about the guys who arrived every day in beat-up trucks and lived-in cars. Most of them just looked homeless and seemed harmless, like they were just happy to be there. The ones I *was* worried about were the guys who lived on the farm full-time—the muscles of the crew. Their only job was to take care of intruders, though I hadn't seen anyone come to the property uninvited. With nothing to do, they entertained themselves by harassing me. I was the only girl there, and their taunting became a daily routine I dreaded. I'd work in the garden, Hope playing in the dirt at my feet, and they'd catcall me, saying nasty things I prayed Hope wouldn't understand. I ignored them. I kept a stony look on my face, but inside, I was crumbling. I didn't like them watching me. I hated the things they said. I felt exposed, unsafe, alone.

Cody was the worst. He never said anything to me, but watched me all the time. Sometimes he'd tell the guys to knock it off when they got too crude, but the way he looked at me made me uneasy. With him, I could tell this was more than entertainment. I felt like his prey, and I tried to avoid him as best as possible.

Things were easier when Jordan was home. When he was nearby, no one acknowledged me. He had no idea what went on when he wasn't home, unaware he was hanging out with predators. I wanted to tell him, but I didn't. Remembering how he reacted when he found Jace's texts in my phone, I knew his jealousy would turn any of my claims against me. But more than that, I saw the way he was around the guys on the farm. These were his boys. I was afraid he'd dismiss my words completely, not believing anything I said about their harassment. If I didn't say anything, he couldn't disappoint me.

Except for Hope, I spent every day by myself. In a way, having her there made me lonelier. I spent the days entertaining her while doing my job, and the evenings cleaning up the house so I could collapse into bed and start again the next day. Occasionally, Jordan and I had time together, but he seemed distant, even when he was in the same room. He had all these friends here, and I had no one. I wanted someone to talk with, someone who could relate with me. I longed for a friend, someone who noticed what I did during the day—not in a leering way, but one that allowed me to believe I existed. I needed a witness to my life. So when a truck came in with two girls in the back, I was curious.

They were dressed differently than I was. That was the first thing I noticed. In the summer heat, shorts and tank tops were a given, but their shorts barely covered their asses, and their tank tops were just a suggestion. I looked down at my clothes—cropped pants and a T-shirt—and felt plain in comparison. While I tried to be as invisible as possible, these girls captured everyone's attention, and it didn't seem to bother them. At least, I thought it didn't until one of them pushed a guy next to her.

"Get the fuck off, or I'll castrate you," she growled, then jumped out of the truck as it lurched to a stop. I studied her, interested at how tough she seemed. She had long black dreads that, even tied back, reached to her waist. A tattoo of an ocean scene covered her arm, and a dragon wrapped around her leg, snaking up her thigh. She wore combat boots, and I imagined if that guy had continued to harass her, he would have known what it felt like to have that boot in his crotch. Her eyes were lined with black, making her blue eyes brilliant as she narrowed them at me. "What the fuck are you looking at?" I looked away, both terrified and in awe.

"Don't mind Eden," the other girl said, hopping down. She gave me a wide smile and stuck out her hand. I took it and she pulled me in. "And don't mind me, I'm a hugger. I'm Bethany." She looked at Hope in the pack on my back. "Who's this?" She gave Hope's foot a tug, who giggled, kicking her feet against my side.

"Ow!" I winced before giving Bethany a sheepish smile. "I'm Maddie, and this is Hope, my daughter."

"She's so cute! She reminds me of my daughter when she was that age."

"You have a kid?" I asked. "Is she here?"

"Oh, hell no. I wouldn't bring my kid to this place." She must have realized how that sounded, because her eyes widened. "I mean, it's fine for you, I'm sure. She's too little to know what's going on here."

"Don't apologize," I told her. "It's not my favorite thing to have her here. I don't even want to... I mean, well, my boyfriend works here. Jordan. But he's usually out in the field."

"Are there other girls here?" Bethany asked.

I shook my head. "You guys are the first. I'm so relieved! It's been hard being the only girl."

"I can imagine. These guys are animals. You have to know how to stand your ground and watch your back, if you know what I mean."

The look she gave me said everything I needed to know. I was good at watching my back. It was the standing my ground part that needed some work. They found my fear enticing. I needed to find my backbone, and quick. I could use a few lessons from Eden, if she'd let me get close to her.

Bethany and Eden were trimmers. According to Bethany, they trimmed drying plants to expose the crystal-covered buds. She used phrases like "bucking the plant" and "giving it a haircut." I felt stupid as she explained everything to me. I had no interest in this lifestyle and I was obviously out of place. Everyone else were scholars in this culture. I was an outsider who knew nothing.

Thankfully, Bethany didn't treat me like I was dumb. She was a couple years older than me, but I felt like the older one. She was carefree and fearless, and didn't seem to have any worries. I learned her daughter was eight and didn't live with her, but with her mother-in-law. She was working the harvest, hoping she could make enough money to get a place. She figured that once she had a house, she could get her daughter back. I hoped she was right. The way Hope was drawn to her, I knew her daughter must feel the same way.

Bethany was full of light, and possessed both innocence and sexuality. Now that she and Eden were here, the attention once reserved for me was divided among us, but it was different with them. Eden could stop the guys' harassment with a mere look, but Bethany flirted back. After a few days of witnessing the back and forth, along with her eye rolls about it when we were out of their sight, I asked her about it.

"Look, these guys are looking for easy victims," she said. "I don't want to mess with them one bit. They're not looking for a girlfriend, so I figure if I act like I want them, maybe they'll want me less."

"That doesn't make sense."

She sighed, then looked at the sky.

"Fine," she said. "They'll end up taking it anyway. If I just give it to them, then it's not rape. Maybe then they'll leave me alone."

"Bethany..."

"I need to go," she said. She turned and ran back toward the warehouse.

The expression on her face stayed with me the rest of day and into the evening. As I made dinner, I wondered what she meant. It made me shudder to think about what these guys could do.

"Hey, sweets," Jordan said, planting a kiss on the back of my neck. I jumped and turned around, catching my breath when I saw it was him. "What's wrong with you? Were you expecting someone else?"

"What? No. I was thinking, and didn't hear you come in. Where have you been?"

"Thinking? About what?" he asked, ignoring my question. I hadn't seen him in three days, and he was acting like I was the one doing something wrong.

"Why aren't you answering my question?"

"Why aren't you answering mine?" He leaned against the counter for a moment while waiting for my reply, but then lifted Hope when she launched herself at his legs. "Hey, pretty girl, I've missed you!"

"She's missed you, too," I told him. "We both have."

Jordan looked at me, then sighed.

"Look, it's easier sometimes to stay with the crop instead of coming all the way back here, all right? There's a lot of newbies coming in, and they can't be trusted. I have to stay there to not only show them the ropes, but make sure they're not doing anything they're not supposed to."

"And you couldn't call?" I asked. "What's the point of having this big fancy phone if you won't even call to let me know when you'll be late, or when you just won't show up?"

"There's no cell phone reception there." He kissed Hope on the cheek, then set her down to play. She whined to be picked up again. "Come on, Hope, Daddy's tired."

"Hope, go play with your toys," I said, pointing to them. She pouted, looking at Jordan while still holding on to his leg. I picked up a piece of sausage from the food I was cooking and blew on it. When it was cool, I handed it to her. She snatched it from my hand and walked into the living room with her prize. I turned off the burner, and took out the plates.

"You could have radioed in that you were staying there," I said to Jordan.

"Come off it. I was doing my job. Why are you always on my back?"

"I'm never on your back!" I insisted. "I was worried! What if something happened to you out there! How would I know? If you couldn't call from your phone, you could have radioed one of the guys to tell me."

"I told you, I don't want you talking to those guys. And I sure as hell don't want to give them a reason to talk with you."

"Then why are we here?" I yelled. "And why do you leave me alone all day long! If you're so afraid of what they'll do to me, why aren't you here to protect me?"

"They won't do anything to you if you don't give them a reason to," Jordan yelled back.

"What's that supposed to mean? So if one of the guys rapes me, it's my fault?" When he didn't say anything, I shook my head. "Bethany was right," I muttered.

"What was Bethany right about?"

"That it's better to give it to them. After all, they'll just take it anyway."

I didn't see it coming when he slapped my face. The pan I was holding flew from my hand, and the food scattered across the kitchen floor. He grabbed me by the neck and dragged me into the bedroom. I caught a glimpse of Hope's crumpled face, and heard her screaming as he threw me onto the bed.

"You're just like your slut friend," he hissed. "You're probably fucking all of them, aren't you?" His face was an inch away from mine as he held me down. I struggled to get free, turning my head from his. There was no escaping; he had me pinned.

"You're hurting me!" I cried.

"Tell me who he is."

"There's no one!"

"I don't believe you. You wouldn't have said that if you weren't. Who is he?"

"Jordan, stop!" I pleaded. "I told you, there's no one! I don't talk to anyone, I don't do anything, I'm here all by myself. The only time I leave the house is to go to the store. Other than that, I'm living here in this piece of shit hellhole, waiting until we can finally get out of here!"

"I don't fucking believe you!" he screamed into my face. I turned away, tears streaming down my cheeks. "Look at me," he growled, and he gripped his hand on my jaw and forced my face toward his. He breathed heavily, and I braced myself for the next hit. Then, as if a light went on inside him, I saw his face soften, and tears filled his eyes. He let me go, and I scrambled to the other side of the bed, hugging myself into the smallest ball I could.

"Oh, baby, I'm so sorry," he whispered. Hope was still crying in the other room. I could hear her, but I couldn't bring myself to get her. I was too wounded, my insides torn apart. I just wanted to go to sleep and escape what just happened, and yet, I had to bite my tongue to keep from calling Jordan back when he went to get her. I didn't want him near her. I didn't want him near me. When he hurt me, he betrayed me. He was supposed to keep us safe from harm. Instead, he *caused* me harm.

"She's scared," Jordan said as he came back into the room. Hope was pushing against him, her face red as snot ran from her nose. She reached for me, trying to get away from him. "Here, take her." He put her on the bed, and she scrambled to me. I opened my arm, holding her as she cried. In an effort to be strong for her, I focused on being her mother, pushing away the part of me that had just been hurt. I wanted to escape what had happened.

I felt Jordan sit on the bed. He reached over and took my hand. His touch repulsed me. I wanted to pull away, but didn't. I was afraid to make him angry again, especially as I held Hope. Or maybe she was my safety net. Maybe he wouldn't hurt me as I held her. It was a sick thought, one I regretted as soon as I had it. Even if she could keep me safe, I couldn't allow her to be my human shield. I was her protector, not the other way around. Tonight, we'd failed her.

"It was a mistake," Jordan said quietly. "Maddie." I didn't look at him. I couldn't. "I'm so, so sorry. I never should have touched you that way. No one should ever touch you that way."

"I didn't do anything," I whispered, looking down as Hope hugged me. Jordan squeezed my hand. He took my words as an invitation, and pulled me to him. I let him, and I rested under his waiting arm.

"No, you didn't," he agreed. "I'm under so much stress it's hard to see straight. I haven't really slept for three days, and I feel like I'm going crazy. I hate the guys working with me. They're a bunch of kids who need to be supervised all the time. None of them know what they're doing, and I end up doing everything. I'm so tired, I've got nothing left in the tank."

I listened to his reasoning, and tried to shield my heart. I didn't want to give in. But when I felt him shudder against me, it took me by surprise.

"There's no excuse." He pulled away from me. I dared myself to look at his face, seeing his tears. I'd never seen him cry. He wasn't that kind of guy. "I'll understand if you need to leave. I shouldn't have hit you."

He got up and walked out of the room. I stayed there for a few minutes. Hope was breathing deeply against me. She'd fallen asleep. None of us had eaten dinner. I considered waking her, but remembered the food was all over the floor. Still, I couldn't stay in the bedroom. I heard Jordan moving around in the front room, and was curious about what he was doing. *What should I do? Leave him? Make him leave? How was I supposed to feel, to react?*

I finally got up, balancing Hope against me as I went into the front room. Jordan was on his hands and knees in the kitchen, cleaning up the mess. With one hand, I moved some of the toys off Hope's bed, and slowly, carefully laid her down. I let my breath out when she was on the bed, relieved she stayed asleep. Then I went into the kitchen. Without speaking, I wet a cloth, then got on my knees to help clean up the food. We worked in silence, not even looking at each other. When the linoleum was clean, Jordan took the cloth from my hands, and rinsed it in the sink.

"Are you hungry?" he asked. I wanted to say no. I felt like I should have lost my appetite, but I was starving. I nodded. He looked like he wanted to smile at me. I know I wanted to smile at him—not because I was happy, but because smiling was what I always did. But right now, smiling wasn't appropriate.

He pulled a pan out of the cabinet and placed it on the stove. As it heated, he took out eggs and bread, then a few potatoes and an onion. I leaned against the wall, not wanting to stay and unwilling to leave. I let him cook for me, watching as he moved carefully around the kitchen. We stayed silent, partly to keep from waking Hope, and partly because we were in shock. Plus, I was afraid to speak. I knew if I did, I'd betray myself. Either I'd throw myself in his arms, or I'd leave him. I didn't want to do either.

He left the room when the food was ready, coming back with the laundry basket. He placed it upside down on the floor, balancing our plates and silverware on top. He sat down near his plate, and looked up to see if I'd do the same. I sat cross-legged, then scooped a tiny portion of food into my mouth. It was delicious. I was ravenous.

"I'm getting a beer, do you want one?" he asked. I never drank—not because I was too young, but because I was too afraid to get drunk while Hope was under my care. Tonight, though, it was necessary. I nodded, and he leaned back and opened the fridge, pulling out two bottles. He twisted off the caps, tossed them in the garbage, and handed me one. If it had been under normal circumstances, we would have clinked bottlenecks. He probably would have been amused I was drinking his beer. Instead, we both took a swig, drinking as if it were water.

I wasn't quite done when the tears came. Mine, not his. Once they started, they wouldn't stop, making me angrier because they revealed my weakness. It wasn't his abuse that made me weak, it was my tears. Plus, they were falling into the food I still wanted to eat. I tried to hide them, placing my hand over my eyes as I continued eating, but my sniffling gave me away. I heard him scoot away from the laundry basket and crawl toward me. I felt him put his arms around me. The motion made me cry harder. I didn't want him to feel sorry for me; it only made me cry more. Worse, I realized I needed his comfort.

I leaned into him, shaking as I silently sobbed. He rubbed his arms over my back, making shushing noises as he comforted me. He stood, then reached down and picked me up, cradling me in his arms as if I weighed little more than Hope. I buried my face in his chest, feeling the dizzying effect of moving without seeing where I was going. He laid me on our bed, and lay down next to me, wiping away my tears. His lips followed, covering every part of my skin where his hands had hurt me. Then his mouth found mine. He touched me gently at first, as if asking permission.

I didn't want to want him. But I did—I wanted him so much. I needed his gentle touch to erase the pain. I needed him to make me forget, to heal me, to hold me closer than humanly possible.

He read my invitation, crushing his mouth against mine. I pressed back, grabbing at his clothes to bring him closer. We stripped off everything, holding each other the whole time. When his skin was against mine, it wasn't enough. I needed him closer. He entered me, and I kept hold of him, using all my strength to keep his body against mine. His chest pushed on my lungs with each thrust, leaving me breathless. I didn't care if I never breathed again. I felt free. I felt release. I felt.

I felt.

I felt.

We came together. He clutched me as he did, crying out into my neck. My head was free of all burdens. My body felt more alive than it ever had. When he fell against me, he wrapped his arms around me and squeezed. I didn't want him to let go. This was how he was supposed to touch me. The other touch…that was someone else. It wasn't him, and it wasn't me. This right here—this was us.

"I'm sorry," he whispered, kissing the top of my head before rolling to his side. I rolled with him, spooning myself into his embrace.

"Don't be sorry," I whispered back. "Let's not do this again. I don't want to speak about this after tonight." I felt him nod, and he kissed me again. Then we were quiet, waiting to see who would fall asleep first.

5

Hidden

"What happened to your neck?" Bethany asked from the couch as I put Hope's jacket on. Cody had chosen the two of us, plus Ricky and Pete, two of the younger guys, to sell fruits and vegetables at the farmers' market since we were the most innocent looking of the group. I'd gone there before with these guys, but today I felt nervous as Bethany peered at my bruises. I brushed her off, not touching the marks where Jordan's fingers had left circles on my flesh. I had already seen them after he left the house, and had been shocked, running my hand over where he'd clutched me in anger.

"It's nothing," I told her. "I'm just clumsy."

"Your cheek, too. It looks bruised." She leaned closer, and I looked away.

"It's nothing. I just…I fell in the shower. It was dumb. I'll heal." By her expression, I could tell she didn't believe me. *Of course* she didn't believe me. I wouldn't believe me.

"Do you have any makeup?" she asked. I shook my head. All my makeup was in Petaluma. Besides, there was no reason to paint my face here: it would only attract attention. "Wait here."

"We'll be late," I protested.

"No, we won't. This will only take a second."

She ran outside, and the bungalow shook as she went down the ramp. I heard one of the guys calling to her, but she was back in a few minutes.

"I'll have to go fast," she said. "They're getting impatient, and we still have to set up. Thank God this is an afternoon market. I can't handle those early morning ones." She pressed a sponge into some concealer and dabbed it on my cheek. Then she started working on my neck. I was relieved that she said nothing about what really happened, treating me as if this were normal. I knew it wasn't, but was comforted that she acted like it was. The last thing I needed was any kind of judgment, and I'd have crumbled if she'd shown me pity. I wondered if this wasn't her first time being around something like this. I didn't want to ask.

She applied a little blush to my cheeks, and then some mascara. She finished the look with some lip gloss. Leaning back, she smiled as she studied her work.

"Perfect," she said. "You still look like you, but *more* you. Go see."

I went into the bathroom. The bruises were hardly noticeable. The one on my cheek was completely gone, and those on my neck were faint. Someone would have to be looking for them to notice. Even more noticeable was how feminine I looked. It felt like ages since I'd worn makeup. Looking at my reflection, I realized while making me look natural, she'd subtly played up my features. It almost looked like I wasn't wearing makeup, except my skin was flawless, my features a bit more pronounced, and my eyes lined with a light layer of black.

"Do you like it?" Bethany stood in the doorway holding Hope, who was playing with the string on the front of her dress. I loved that Hope was so comfortable around her. I was, too; I finally had an ally. She'd only been here a week, but I felt like we'd known each other forever.

"I love it. Do you have more I could borrow?"

"Keep all that. I brought a small beauty store in my bag. I have plenty more." She leaned closer, scrutinizing my cheek. "The next time you, uh, fall, or whatever, apply something cool to the area. Like frozen peas, or something. It helps with the swelling."

"There won't be a next time. I'll be more careful."

"Whatever," she said. A shadow crossed her expression, but soon she was smiling again, bouncing Hope on her hip. "We'd better go, or they'll leave without us."

We didn't have a lot of time once we got to the park where they held the Saturday market. Most vendors had their booths set up under tents. We hurriedly propped up our canopy and unfolded the tables. Ricky and Pete carried over heavy boxes of produce while Bethany and I set up the display. We were sweating by the time we were done, and people began to trickle into the market. I wiped my brow, smearing concealer on my arm.

"So much for my makeup."

"Did you bring any with you?" Bethany asked.

"I didn't even think to," I admitted. She took some foundation from her purse and reapplied it under my eye.

"Don't wipe your face anymore. Dab it if you need to, but try to keep from touching your cheek or neck. The bruises are showing."

I touched my face anyway, suddenly self-conscious. She grabbed my hand.

"It's hardly noticeable. If anything, it looks like you have a little dirt on your face."

"Great. People will think I forgot how to bathe."

"Or that you work on a farm," Bethany said. "It's not that bad."

I didn't have time to worry about how I looked. Once the market kicked into high gear, we were too busy selling and restocking. Hope was content in the carrier on my back, flirting with customers as we handed out bags of produce. She was a natural people magnet.

Ricky and Pete disappeared as soon as they'd unpacked the van. I was used to this. The other times I'd worked the market, they'd stumbled back, bleary-eyed, when it was time to close up and head back to the farm. I didn't like riding in a truck while one of them drove high, but we always made it back in one piece.

"Maddie?" I turned and felt my cheeks get red when I saw Erin, a girl I knew from high school. I hadn't known her well, but we shared a few classes. "Oh my God, it *is* you! And your little girl! How *are* you?"

"Erin, hi," I said, wanting to shrink under the table. "I'm good. What are you doing all the way up here?"

"My family's on a camping trip," she said. "We came to buy some food. What about you? You're a vendor here?"

"Uh, yeah," I said. "I live here now. I'm working on a farm."

"That's so cool, and they let your daughter work with you. What's her name again?"

"This is Hope," I said, turning so she could get a better view. I felt Hope shift behind me, and I knew she was doing the shy flirtation thing.

"Oh man, what happened to your neck?" Erin asked. Then her eyes widened. "Oh, sorry." I realized with a start that she thought they were hickeys, not bruises. I moved my hair around my neck, as if it would cover the marks, and gave an embarrassed laugh.

"They're not hickeys. I fell in the shower. It looks worse than it is."

"You must have hit your cheek, too," she said. As soon as she said it, a look of realization washed over her face.

"Can I interest you in some peach slices?" Bethany asked behind me. She gently moved me out of the way and held a plate with fruit on it. "They were just picked this morning." Erin looked at Bethany and shook her head, and then looked back at me.

"It was good seeing you," I said quickly. "Have fun on your camping trip." I hurried to the truck before she could answer, pretending I needed to do something. Hope was getting heavy, anyway. I unbuckled the pack, and balanced her on the truck seat so I could release my arms from the straps. Once we were free, I gave her a couple pieces of fruit, and then checked the mirror. I glared at my reflection. The makeup barely muted the purple marks. There were dark shadows under my eyes, and I was sure I'd lost weight since the last time Erin saw me. I looked like a wreck, and she probably assumed I was strung out or in an abusive relationship.

"Who cares what she thinks," I whispered. I knew the truth.

"Who was that girl, some cheerleader friend of yours?" Bethany asked when I came back to the front of our booth, Hope secured to my back once again.

"Hardly. We weren't friends; we just went to school together."

"I gathered that. She doesn't seem like the type of girl you'd hang out with."

"Oh? What's my type?" I asked, amused.

"I don't know. Not perky, like her. Someone who's more reserved or something. Maybe reads a lot of books and does well on tests."

"A nerd, right?"

She shook her head.

"Not a nerd. Maybe a cool geek, though, like the girls who can rock Doc Martens and thick-rimmed glasses, with a Harry Potter novel in their bags."

"I guess," I said. "I didn't have a lot of friends in high school. At least, not after I became pregnant with Hope. Kind of hard to make friends when you have a kid."

"I know how that goes," Bethany said. "But I dropped out when I got pregnant, and never went back."

"You could, you know," I said. "Take night classes, maybe."

"True, but what's the point?" The market was dying down, and she started carrying produce bins back to the truck. I followed with another tray. I was getting hungry, and anxious to be done so I could hide in the house the rest of the day.

"The point is, you could do anything with your life, not just this," I said. "Haven't you wanted to do more than work on some guy's pot farm?"

She paused. "I always wanted to be a writer," she said after a while. "I have all these stories in my head, and sometimes it feels like they're real. I've written a few of them down, but I haven't finished any." She looked at me and grinned. "It's silly, though. Nobody makes money writing books, unless they're J.K. Rowling."

"You never know," I said. "Even J.K. Rowling was a poor single mom with a dream before Harry Potter."

"I guess," Bethany said. "But until then, I'm just a trimmer."

***

When Jordan came back that night, he told me to put on a sweatshirt and join him outside. From the window, I saw some of the guys starting a bonfire in a pit near the warehouse, while others pulled around chairs. Bethany was there, laughing with some guy smoking a cigarette.

I didn't want to leave Hope alone in the house, but Jordan assured me we'd only be a few feet away.

"It's like being in our own backyard while the kid is asleep. I'm sure your parents did that when you were little. She'll be fine." I slipped on a sweatshirt and followed him out the door, though I hated the idea of leaving her on her own.

"I'm checking on her every fifteen minutes," I told him.

"Suit yourself, but you know she stays asleep once she's down." I knew he was right.

"This is nice, huh?" he said, squeezing my knee once we were sitting by the fire. Because we hadn't seen each other all day, it had been easy to forget what happened the night before. But now I felt the tension between us. I knew by the way he took my hand and played with my fingers that he felt bad. Normally he'd be hanging with the guys on his own, but tonight he was being attentive and kind, forgetting about his friends as he stayed with me. "Can I get you something to drink?"

"Maybe a soda," I said. He got up and grabbed a can out of the cooler, along with a beer for himself. Bethany was nearby, leaning against the warehouse while Cody was whispering something in her ear.

"Here you go, babe," Jordan said.

"Thanks." I watched Bethany, waiting to see would happen. She kept glancing at the ground while Cody talked. She smiled when he looked at her. But when his eyes weren't on her face, her expression fell. It was clear she was uncomfortable, and when he took her hand and pulled her into the warehouse, I got up to follow.

"Where are you going?" Jordan asked, grabbing my arm. I jerked away out of instinct, mostly because of how Cody's possessive grasp on my friend made me feel. I realized in an instant how that must have looked, and sat back down.

"Um, nowhere," I said. But I couldn't stop thinking about Bethany, wondering what I should do. I knew she didn't want this, but also wouldn't stop it from happening. I needed to step in, but I didn't know how. I shifted in my seat, glancing at the warehouse.

"What's wrong with you?" Jordan asked.

"It's Bethany. She's with Cody."

"And that bothers you?"

"Well, yeah," I said. His face darkened and I shook my head. "Stop that," I told him. "I don't like him. It's not like that. It's just that she doesn't like him either. I think she's in trouble."

"Bullshit," Jordan said. "That girl has been begging to get laid since she got here. Cody's just giving her what she wants."

I scowled, starting to get up again. He took hold of me and didn't let go.

"Leave them alone. They're adults. If Bethany doesn't want it, she'll let him know. Cody's a good guy; she could do worse."

I disagreed. All the times he'd looked at me, I felt like he was sizing me up, trying to figure out how much of a challenge I'd be. Bethany had already shown how little fight she'd give. She'd made herself an easy target.

"I need to stop this."

"Don't be a cock block." He kept his hand on my arm, squeezing it this time. I wanted to pull away, but didn't want to cause a scene. As I sat, my mind stayed with Bethany. A joint came our way, and Jordan took a long drag before handing it to me. I'd never smoked before, and wasn't going to start now. He shrugged when I refused, and leaned over to pass it to the guy closest to me. Then he turned to talk with a group of guys to his right. Once again, I was on my own.

"I'm going to check on Hope." I touched him on the arm to get his attention. He looked at me and nodded, then went back to his conversation.

Everything was quiet in the house. I heard laughter from the bonfire, coupled with Hope's deep breathing. I moved closer to her, watching her sleep. Jordan had been right; she was out for the night.

I was tempted to stay where I was, to avoid the party and call it a night. Maybe stay in bed and play on my phone. I'd recently created a Facebook account under a fake name, and used it sometimes to check up on things in Petaluma. Mostly, it was to see what Jace was doing. I kept promising myself I'd stop looking him up. I was afraid I'd log on one day and discover he'd met someone new. I knew I shouldn't let it bother me if he did. After all, *I'd* moved on. Still, I dreaded finding out, which, of course, had me visiting his page even more.

Jordan probably wouldn't miss me if I stayed inside, which meant this was the perfect moment to go check on Bethany. One last glance at Hope's sleeping body, and I crept back out of the house. I walked wide around the bonfire, keeping my eyes on Jordan. He was too busy talking to notice me. I made it to the warehouse and slipped inside. I thought I was alone, but caught my breath when I saw Eden sitting in the corner, smoking a cigarette.

"I didn't see you there," I said. She stared at me silently. "Have you seen Bethany?" Still, she said nothing. She took a long drag, the glow at the end traveling toward her lips, then she blew the smoke out, a steady stream penetrating the air around her before she dropped the cigarette and crushed it with her foot. When she leaned back in the chair, I could see she wouldn't be any help. I started toward the door that led to the back rooms.

"Don't go in there," Eden said.

"Is she in there?" I asked. She stared again. I felt frustrated. But then she lost a bit of her hardened look.

"You don't want to get involved."

"Actually, I *do*," I said. "She's my friend."

"Yeah, but sometimes you need to think of yourself before you think of others. What do you think will happen if you open that door and come upon something you don't want to see? What happens if you become a part of the problem instead of the solution?"

I clenched and unclenched my fists. I felt powerless. If it were me, I was sure Bethany would step in. Or *would* she? She knew Jordan had hit me, but she didn't tell me to leave him. Instead, she helped me cover up the mess. Maybe that was all she wanted from me, too. That didn't sit well with me.

"You know she doesn't want this," I said. "Cody is a bad guy. She thinks she doesn't deserve more than this, but she's wrong. I need to stop him before it's too late."

I turned toward the door, and was almost hit as it opened. Cody came out, his shirt opened and he paused as he saw me. He gave me a wry smile, leaning close to me. I realized what Eden had been saying, and shrank back.

"Ladies," Cody said with a nod, then headed back to the bonfire. I glanced at Eden, then ran through the open door. There was a hallway with only one door open at the end. I raced toward it and came upon Bethany lying on the couch. She was naked from the waist down, her eyes glazed, a belt looped around her arm, and a needle on the ground.

"I'll get her some pants," Eden said. I didn't know she'd followed me, but was grateful she had.

We dressed Bethany and carried her back to the dorms in the warehouse. There were rows of bunks, and Eden led me to the one she shared with Bethany. We laid her on the bottom bed and covered her. She mumbled something, but I couldn't understand what she said.

"Let her sleep it off," Eden said. I started to protest, but she touched my arm. The move shocked me, silencing me. Eden didn't touch anyone, or let anyone come close enough to touch her. She was usually so terrifying, completely unapproachable. But tonight, she was in this with me. "She'll be fine," she said.

"Shouldn't we take her to the hospital?" I asked. "At least call someone?"

"Who will we call? We're nobodies, and no one cares." She sighed as I remained unsure. "She'll be fine. I'll keep an eye on her and make sure no one touches her. If it seems like she's in trouble, I'll make one of these pricks drive us to the hospital. But I promise you she's fine, and will be normal in the morning."

I nodded, and started to leave. But then I turned back. I had to know.

"Why didn't you stop him?" I asked. Her tired eyes stared through me. But then I saw it before she looked away—*shame.*

"I didn't want to become part of the problem."

6

Three

Summertime ended, and so did harvest. With the colder weather, workers began to leave the farm. Even Bethany went, just as I knew she would. I wasn't prepared for it, though. As Eden said, Bethany was fine the day after the bonfire. She was different, though. She still laughed, but her smile never reached her eyes. I'd sensed she was counting down the days when she'd finally be free of this place. Still, both of us sobbed as we hugged goodbye, promising to keep in touch. I hoped she meant it.

Eden was one of the few who stayed behind. Even after that night with Bethany, we weren't exactly friends—but we weren't enemies, either. We shared a mutual respect, then stayed out of each other's way.

My relationship with Jordan changed, too. I often looked back at the first few days we lived on the farm, amused at how naive I'd been. Once the shock of living in a shack on a pot farm wore off, I'd found some comfort in the routine of living as a family. It was like playing house, except it was real. I cooked for him after a long day of work, and we fell into bed every night, making love before falling asleep.

But I was a shell of who I used to be.

Jordan was often gone for several days at a time, and I lived for those days. I could relax, knowing no one was looking over my shoulder, accusing me of flirting, cheating, even thinking about other guys. If I glanced at any of the workers, he assumed I was messing around while he was gone. I became a pro at keeping my eyes trained to the ground.

Though I was glad when Jordan was gone, I also dreaded it. As only one of two girls on the farm, I was always on edge. I remained guarded, but was more confident than before—it served well as a shield. The guys were less likely to treat me as an object when I made myself appear as less of a victim. I took my cues from Eden, refusing to back down when they leered at me. I pretended they didn't exist, letting their name-calling and mocking roll off me. I hid my innocence with dark eyeliner, practicing hardened looks in the mirror before using them outside. I still couldn't look them in the eyes, though. Jordan's accusations had me living in fear, worrying that anything I did might invite attention. I became the ice queen. At first, this amused the guys, but when I didn't back down from their catcalls, they grew tired of it.

Except for Cody. His eyes still followed me wherever I went. When I dared to look at him, he met me with an amused expression, as if telling me he'd take what he wanted when he decided it was time. I only hoped Jordan and I could leave before that time came.

The thing was, my dreams of leaving with Jordan were changing. I no longer fantasized about the farm we'd tend as a family. Instead, I dreamed of leaving him and this place forever, never looking back. I just didn't know how to leave. My car sat in the corner of the compound on cinder blocks, its wheels leaning against the warehouse, taunting me. Jordan had removed the wheels the month before, after I threatened to leave him. He'd seen me laughing with Ricky earlier that day as we pulled in from an afternoon at the farmers' market. He hadn't even asked questions. First he came at Ricky, accusing him of messing with me. Then, when Ricky insisted there was nothing going on, Jordan hit me across the face in front of everyone. He dragged me back to the house, leaving Hope outside. I saw Eden pick Hope up as Jordan shoved me into the house, shouting accusations. I no longer submitted to his abuse, though. I fought back, telling him to go to hell, that he was out of his mind, that I was leaving him the next chance I got with my own damn car, to which he promised to kill everyone who helped me leave, including anyone I ran to in Petaluma. Then he removed the car's wheels and hid the bolts that night, leaving us both with no way off this horrible farm.

My other issue was Hope. She adored Jordan, and he adored her. She'd grown immune to our fighting, and wouldn't even look up when we screamed at each other. She was no longer scared of him when he'd shove me or I shoved back. It was as if she couldn't see it happening, as if she were in her own world while we raged at each other. She didn't see him as the monster I did. Instead, he was her favorite person in the world. She'd launch herself at him in the morning, and wouldn't leave his side. He looked at her with adoration and spoke to her with love—but not to me. I fought feelings of jealousy over a toddler who deserved to feel loved by her daddy. Still, I wished there was someone who looked at me that way.

When Jordan was gone, I continued to look Jace up on Facebook and see what he was doing. Sometimes I felt like he kept his profile open on purpose, as if he knew I was checking in on him. There were pictures of him smiling, a few of him with Kayci, and status updates about college. His photos made me both happy and sad. I was glad to see he was doing well, but I no longer fit into his life. What would he do with a girl like me? I was damaged goods, broken, cased by a hardened shell. I knew I had issues he couldn't fix. Seeing his perfect smile, his perfect world, his perfect life, I knew I couldn't be near him and mess all that up.

I thought about Charlie, too, mostly agonizing over my last words to him. I knew he'd never forgive me. I didn't deserve his forgiveness. I had no place to go if I ever got the courage to leave. My disabled car wasn't keeping me here, it was my lack of options. I'd burned all my bridges.

***

I got a break on the morning of Hope's birthday. I'd saved the money Cody paid me, but without a car, I had no way to get her presents or a cake. I'd begged Jordan to fix the car, and he kept putting me off. But that morning, he tossed a ring of keys on the bed as I was waking up.

"What's this?"

"Keys to the truck," he said. "I don't have time to put the wheels back on the car, so I asked Cody to let you borrow the truck. He said it was okay as long as you put gas in it."

I sat up and grabbed the keys before he could change his mind.

"Thank you!"

"Don't say I never did anything for you," he said with a wink. I was tempted to remind him that he was the one who took the wheels off my car in the first place. However, I wasn't about to mess up my chance of getting off the farm for a few hours.

Hope was still asleep, so I took a quick shower and put on some makeup. When I was done, Jordan had already made breakfast for all of us, and they were sitting at the table he'd brought home a few weeks back.

"There's my birthday girl!" I exclaimed. She squealed as I covered her in kisses.

"Mama, it's my birfday!"

"I know! Do you know how old you are today?" She looked at her fingers, and then held up three just like we'd practiced for the past couple of weeks.

"I'm two!" she said.

"No, baby, you're three. And if you finish your breakfast, we can go to the park and play today."

"With KK?" she asked. My heart skipped a beat, even though Jordan had no idea who KK was. But why did she even mention her? We hadn't seen Kayci or Jace in almost four months. I ignored her question, pretending I didn't hear it. "Mama, we see KK?"

"Who's KK?" Jordan asked.

"Just some friend we used to see in Petaluma." I didn't elaborate, and was relieved when he didn't ask any other questions.

As soon as Hope was done eating, I dressed her in overalls and a long-sleeved shirt. Her hair was long enough to make pigtails, and I played with her curls while she giggled. It was chilly outside, so I grabbed her jacket. From the many times Ricky had driven us to the market in the truck, I knew it took forever for the heater to kick in. Because I didn't have a jacket of my own, I layered up two sweatshirts. I wasn't sure what I'd do when winter came, but for now, this would work.

***

"Don't stay out too long," Jordan said when I gave him a kiss on the cheek. He said it with a smile, but I couldn't help taking it as a warning. *Don't take too long, or I'll think you're cheating on me. Don't take too long, or I'll send someone out to find you. Don't take too long, or you'll be sorry.*

"I'll do my best," I told him. "But I'd like to take Hope to the park like I promised. We could use some time away from the farm."

He stared at me a moment. Knowing his jealousy, I faked a smile and turned to leave. When I glanced back, he nodded.

"That will be fun for Hope, and it will give me a chance to catch a nap."

Hope held my purse while I carried her car seat from my car to the truck. Out of the corner of my eye, I saw Cody watching me from the warehouse doorway. I didn't want to look in his direction, but I did, keeping my eyes low as I nodded my thanks for letting me borrow the truck. I buckled Hope into her car seat, then slipped into the driver's seat. The truck sprang to life when I turned the key in the ignition, and we both jerked in the cab as I figured out the gears. I nodded again at the guys manning the gate as I rolled past. Then, after ten minutes of driving on the winding dirt road, I hit the pavement and headed into town.

I was free…at least for a few hours.

It felt strange to drive again. I could go anywhere, do anything, and I had no one to tell me when I had to return. Except, I did. Jordan might have stayed back at the farm, but I felt his presence. I knew if I took too long, he'd start blowing up my phone. I was tempted to turn it off, but that would only cause more trouble once I got back. For now, I hoped he'd leave us alone, let us be Maddie and Hope, mother and daughter —the way things were back when I thought I'd never see him again.

I turned the radio and cracked the window to let in some of the cool October air. Hope sat beside me in her too-small car seat. She nodded her head to the beat while looking out the window, pretending she knew the song even though neither of us had heard it before. I couldn't believe how fast she was growing. It seemed strange how much things had changed in the past three years. It felt like such a short time since I'd held her for the first time, her tiny body wrapped in a sweatshirt as I found her name. *Hope.* I hadn't had a lot of hope before that moment. But as soon as I looked into her face, it was like everything made sense.

Even though I'd thought it was my only option, I still felt shame over almost giving her up. I figured I had nothing to give her. As soon as I held her, I fell in love. I loved her more than I'd ever loved anything. I wanted more for her than the life I was living. I wanted her to have a home, two parents who loved her, and a comfortable bed to sleep in. I never wanted her to know what it was like to be hungry or homeless. I wanted her to go to school and blend in with the other kids, to take for granted everything she was given because it came so easily. I wanted her to live a good life, a wonderful life.

A life I couldn't give her.

Without Charlie, she wouldn't have been sitting next to me. I would have missed so much—the sound of her laugh, how funny she was, how her eyes lit up when she saw someone she loved. If I'd left her at the firehouse, I wouldn't know any of this. Because of Charlie, I got to be her mom.

I missed him. It had been four months since I left his house—four months since I betrayed him. The longer I was gone, the more I knew I could never go back.

I was no better than his daughter.

Charlie told me about Ellie, and the tragic way he and Viola lost her. The Winstons did everything for their little girl. Life was perfect. But things changed when Ellie started dating. She fell in love with a guy they knew was bad news. She became pregnant, and took off. *We only wanted the best for her,* Charlie told me. *But maybe we were too hard on her, pushing her too much.*

Months later, they heard something in Charlie's workshop. Thinking it was an animal, he grabbed his rifle to scare it off. Instead, it was an intruder, and Charlie fired as the figure came toward him. One thief was hit; the other got away.

When I turned on the light, it was Ellie, Charlie told me. She'd died instantly, and his guilt magnified his grief.

When he first told me the story, I thought Ellie was terrible. She'd been so awful to him and Viola. I thought she was lucky to have a mom and dad who loved her, especially since my parents had kicked me out when they found I was pregnant. I wanted everything Ellie had taken for granted.

But when I got it, I threw it all away. If Charlie had it in his heart to forgive me, I didn't deserve it. Even if I returned, I doubted he'd ever speak to me again.

I pulled into the parking lot of the local park, and Hope kicked her feet when she saw where we were. The playground was empty, probably due to the colder weather.

"I guess only bad moms take their kids outside to play in 50-degree weather," I said to Hope, unbuckling her. As soon as she was on the ground, she ran to the play structure in the center of the park. I closed the door and raced after her, chasing her around the playground as she laughed. For the next half-hour, I pushed her on the swings, watched her slip down the slide, and created clumsy castles in the sand. A couple more families came, bringing kids around Hope's age. After the usual awkwardness among the kids, they were soon playing games with each other, and I was free to kick back. The other moms knew each other, and the last thing I wanted to do was to talk to anyone. So I took out my phone and pretended to look at it. But looking at it made my fingers twitch. Soon, I had the Facebook app uploaded, and I searched for Jace's name using my fake profile. What I saw made me smile.

"HBD Hope."

It was his latest status update, and a clue that he probably knew I was looking. He'd remembered her birthday, even though I'd only told him once when we were getting to know each other. I glanced through his latest photos. He hadn't posted any new ones, but I looked through them anyway until they made me feel lonely. I logged off and deleted the app so Jordan couldn't see what I'd been doing. Then I punched in Charlie's number. I didn't know why. I couldn't call him, and looking at the numbers made me miss him that much more.

"I'll hang up if he answers," I whispered, hitting the call button. The phone rang in my ear. *What are you doing? What are you doing? What are you doing?*

"Hello, you've reached Charlie and Viola Winston." I smiled as I heard Charlie's voice on the answering machine, but my heart ached. He hadn't updated the message, even though she'd died months ago. "We're not in right now, but if you leave your name and number, we'll get back to you soon." I hung up as the beep sounded. His voice stayed with me, though. It was a warm blanket, representing the love, safety, and security I longed for. Why had I ever left?

I watched Hope playing, ashamed of our current living situation. She laughed as she ran, holding hands with her new friend. I wished I could feel as happy as she was. I'd forgotten how to laugh, or what it felt like to be free. I was shackled in this life, and there was no way out.

I redialed Charlie's number, needing to hear his voice again. It rang twice, then the phone clicked.

"Hello?" I panicked and hung up the phone. I felt my heart race as I realized my error. Now Jordan could find out. Charlie could call me back. He could find me. Jordan would see the number on our cellphone bill. That would lead to Jordan hurting me, or worse, hurting Charlie.

I stared at my phone, waiting to see if he'd call. Nothing happened. He wasn't calling back.

"Hope, it's time to leave," I called out. She ignored me and kept playing. Sighing, I got up and joined her on the playground. "We have to go," I told her.

"No, Mama," Hope complained, pulling away from me as I took her hand.

"Don't you want to get your present?" I asked her. She paused, and then looked at me. "And your birthday cake?" She ran from the park, not even saying goodbye to her new friends.

The toy store was packed, kids running around, moms and dads following close behind. I felt awkward and out of place. I'd become so antisocial. Even at the farmers' market, I got anxious just knowing I'd be around people. I had a hard time looking at anyone, afraid they might be spying on me for Jordan. The feeling was no different here. I kept my eyes low, careful not to even smile at anyone who looked in my direction. What if Jordan was testing me? What if he had someone follow me to see if I might flirt with them or show interest? I knew it was crazy, but knowing Jordan, I couldn't put it past him.

We searched the store for the perfect doll, one with long brown hair she could brush. The doll we found even came with an extra outfit. I winced when the checker told me the price, but handed over three twenties. With the change, I took Hope to the grocery store and picked up a box of cupcakes. She wanted ones that looked like Halloween, which was lucky since that was all they had. We chose ones with orange frosting piled high, topped with black sprinkles shaped like bats. Once I paid, we headed back to the farm.

***

I was careful with the cupcakes the whole ride, setting them between us and leaving one hand on top in between shifting gears. At every turn, I held my breath, sure they'd slip off the seat, but managed to make it back with the box secure. Once Hope was unbuckled and on the ground, I slung my purse over my shoulder, picked up the car seat with one hand, and then reached over to retrieve the cupcakes. The box slipped from my hand and landed lid down.

"No!" I shuffled everything I was carrying, and bent down clumsily for the box, afraid to see the damage.

"Hold up, I got it." I turned as a guy I'd never seen before moved around me and picked up the box. "Well, I'm sure they still taste good," he said, looking at me with a grin. The light color of his gray eyes contrasted with his dark skin, and an electric current flowed through me as I returned the smile. My face felt hot, and I realized two things—I was looking at him, and he was absolutely breathtaking.

"I'm Ashton," he said, sticking out his free hand. "Cody's cousin."

I was unsure what to do with his outstretched hand. Yes, shake it, but it was more contact than I allowed any of the other guys. He reached over and took my hand that covered my purse and shook it for me. I looked down, still smiling.

"I know what you're thinking," he continued.

"You do?"

"Yes. You're wondering how someone as ugly as Cody can have a cousin as handsome and charming as me."

"That's not what I thought at all," I said. "I wondered how you two could be related when…" I nodded my head at Ashton's bare arm. He looked down, then back at me, pretending to be shocked. I rolled my eyes.

"You mean, why I'm black when he's white?" he asked. He gave an exaggerated shake of his head, sighing.

"What?" I asked.

"I was hoping you had a less predictable question. Something like, what's your sign, or when are you free for dinner. Right now, by the way."

My breath caught in my chest, and I realized I was in a dangerous situation. He was flirting with me, and I was letting it happen. If Jordan overheard any of this, he'd go ballistic. Ashton and touched my arm and I jerked away.

"Hey, relax. I was just messing with you," he said. "I know you're Jordan's girl. Cody told me all about you."

I wanted to ask more, like, *what* Cody said so I could set Ashton straight, but I'd already dug myself into a hole. He was attractive, I enjoyed his flirting, and if Jordan found out, I was going to pay.

"Thanks for picking up the cupcakes," I said, taking the box from him.

"I can carry them for you. It looks like you have your hands full." He nodded at the car seat in my other hand. I was determined not to make the same mistake twice, in all ways.

"I got it, thanks. Nice to meet you." I turned to walk to my car so I could put the car seat inside. Hope raced to catch up with me, holding her doll as she ran. I gave her a smile when I looked down at her, but raised an eyebrow as she returned a serious look.

"What's up, baby?" I asked her.

"I'm telling Daddy," she said.

7

Hey

I wasn't sure I heard her right. *Telling Daddy? Seriously?*

"What are you talking about?" I asked her as we reached the car. I put the car seat inside, and then shut the door and leaned on it.

"I'm telling that you were talking to that man," she said. Then she ran toward the bungalow. I felt sick to my stomach. All this time I'd worried that Jordan had stationed spies to watch me and report back to him. I hadn't known the spy was my own daughter.

"Hope, wait!" I shouted. She stopped and turned, waiting for me to catch up. "Honey, there's nothing wrong with talking with the people who work here at the farm."

"But Daddy doesn't want you to talk to boys."

"He doesn't want me to be mean, either, right?" She shook her head. "Don't you think it's a good idea to be nice to people?" She nodded. "It's okay for me to talk to the other people who live here because they're our neighbors."

"Won't Daddy get mad?" I smiled and squeezed her into a hug.

"No, but he will if we don't share our cupcakes with him." She laughed as I pretended to eat her cheeks. "Let's go see if he's up from his nap." I set her down and followed her, carrying the box of smooshed cupcakes. I was smiling, but inside, I was fuming. *How dare he brainwash her!* I knew it wasn't her fault, but I felt betrayed. I'd given up everything for her. My whole life had been turned upside down for her. I sacrificed everything so she could be first. But her loyalty was with Jordan, a man who controlled me with fear and force.

"She's only three," I whispered, bringing myself back to reality. She didn't know what she was doing. She was a sponge, soaking up everything in her environment. This was all Jordan's fault. *No. Not all of it.* I was to blame, too.

Was this how I wanted Hope to be raised? Was I really going to let my fear keep me here? Every day I stayed was another lesson for Hope—women were property, we couldn't control our sexuality, we couldn't be trusted, and we didn't deserve a life of our own. Allowing Hope to grow up this way was not okay.

Then why is it okay for me?

"Took you long enough. I was beginning to think you got lost," Jordan said as we came in the house. I started to glare at him, but caught myself when I saw his smile. "Did you guys have fun?"

"I got a baby!" Hope exclaimed, racing to her dad so she could show him. He scooped her up in his arms, and took the doll she handed him.

"She looks just like you," he said. "Wait, I can't tell you apart. Hope, is that you?" he asked the doll. "You're so little!"

"Daddy!" she said.

"Hold on, baby doll, I'm talking to Hope," he told her, and then turned back to the doll.

"Daddy, I'm Hope!" she insisted. He looked at her, back at the doll, and then back at her.

"You can't be Hope, because Hope gets the birthday present I got for her."

"Me Daddy! I'm Hope!"

"Are you sure?"

I relaxed as he teased her, especially when he looked in my direction and gave me a wink. The anger I'd felt earlier washed away as he charmed our daughter. I was overreacting; she was a three-year-old who didn't know what she was saying.

"Ready for your surprise?" he asked. He put her down, and she followed him outside.

"What are you up to?" I asked.

"You'll see. You're going to love this."

He led us to the warehouse and told us to wait outside. He went in, and I heard a whirring noise before he came back out. First came the ride-on car, then Jordan pushing it. Hope squealed, dropping her doll on the ground as she raced to the car.

My heart sank. We had discussed gifts and decided the doll would be her big present. When he said he wanted to get her a little something from just him, I thought he meant a doll accessory, hair clips, maybe a new outfit. I didn't know he meant an expensive motorized car.

I picked the doll up and brushed it off. Then I watched as Jordan showed Hope how the car worked. She was a fast learner, and was soon driving it around the parking lot. A few of the guys came out to watch, laughing as Hope squealed while she drove. Out of the corner of my eye, I noticed Ashton was one of them. It took everything I had not to look at him.

"Do you see that guy?" Jordan asked, nodding toward Ashton. I still didn't look, but nodded. "He thinks he's such a big deal just because he's Cody's cousin. Last night was his first night here, but he was calling shots like he owned the place." He turned and glared in Ashton's direction. I continued looking at the ground. "I mean, they don't even look alike. How can they be related?"

I didn't know what I should say. I was sure whatever I said, he'd see through me. He'd know I'd talked with Ashton earlier, looked him in the eye, and found him attractive. He'd know everything by the way I formed my words. So I kept silent. Luckily, Jordan didn't seem to expect a response. He went back to Hope, chasing her around the lot while she drove. I slipped away, taking the forgotten doll with me.

***

We had macaroni and cheese—Hope's favorite—for dinner that night. I made it like my mom used to make, extra creamy with pieces of hot dog and broccoli. When I was a kid, this was the only way I'd eat my vegetables. I realized, watching Hope put a piece of broccoli in her mouth, this was my mother's way of making my junk food somewhat healthy.

For *me*, this was my way of stretching our food budget. It didn't matter how hard we worked, there never seemed to be extra money. I'd never had to pay bills or create a budget, so I let Jordan be in charge. This meant whenever I got paid, I handed him the money. In return, he made sure we had food and our cellphone bill was paid. We always had food to eat and our phones still worked, so he was living up to his end of the bargain. But I couldn't help feeling bitter about the expensive toy he bought for Hope when I thought we didn't have the money. Did we have more than I thought? Was he holding out on me?

When we were done, I set the plates in the sink to soak, then brought out the cupcakes from the refrigerator. I'd tried to fix the frosting, but they looked pretty bad. Jordan raised an eyebrow when he saw them.

"I dropped them on my way to the house," I explained, my guilt over my interaction with Ashton weighing heavy on me. I pushed it aside, focusing on my clumsiness instead. I felt like such an idiot, like I couldn't do anything right. My gift for Hope was lame. The cupcakes were ruined. We lived in a shack on a pot farm. I gave up everything for this life.

"They look boo-tiful," Jordan quipped. I rolled my eyes at his lame Halloween joke, and put an orange and black cupcake in front of each of us. I'd forgotten candles—another failure—so we just sang Happy Birthday to Hope before eating dessert.

When she was finished, there was frosting on her face and hands, even in her hair. I picked her up and stripped her in the tub. She played with her boats while I washed her hair and rinsed out the suds. Once her fingers looked like prunes, I let out the water and wrapped her in a towel. I got her ready for bed, kissed her goodnight, and tucked her new doll in with her.

"Car too, Mama," she said. I shook my head.

"The car stays outside," I told her. "Besides, it won't fit under the blankets." She giggled as I poked at her ribs. Then she talked me into a bedtime story. I curled up next to her and made up my own version of *Sleeping Beauty*, telling of a princess in a faraway castle being guarded by a dragon, waiting for a prince to wake her up and rescue her. Once I reached the happily ever after, she was quiet and her eyes looked droopy.

"Goodnight, Princess," I kissed her cheek, then watched her after she closed her eyes. It was amazing how adaptable kids were. Here she was, sleeping on a futon in the living room of a drafty bungalow, and this was normal to her. I had a long way to go before any of this felt normal.

Jordan was lying on the bed, watching a show on his phone when I came in. I changed into sweats, then sat next to him. He never even looked up from his screen. I pulled out my journal, but everything I wanted to write was about him—how frustrated I was that he showed me up with Hope's car, how I hated it here and wanted to leave, how I never expected things to be this terrible. I couldn't write any of that. I never wrote anything negative about Jordan; I didn't know if he read my journal when I wasn't looking. So instead, I usually wrote about how Hope and I spent our days. It took away the whole purpose of journaling, and was one more chain in this imprisoning relationship. At least it was some form of recording my days.

Tonight, though, it wasn't happening. I needed to get these feelings out somehow or I'd be pissed all night.

"Can we talk?" He glanced over at me, and then back at his phone.

"This is almost over; give me fifteen minutes."

I narrowed my eyes as he ignored me. "Never mind," I said. I turned off the light, then pulled back the covers and climbed in. With a sigh, I rolled over to go to sleep.

"What's the matter?" Jordan asked.

"It's not important. Go back to watching your show. I'm going to sleep." This time, it was his turn to sigh. I felt him move, hearing the sound of his phone as he put it on the floor. He spooned me, his body fitting perfectly behind mine, and put his arm around me to pull me closer. I tried to remain stubborn, but melted into his embrace. It was a warmer alternative than holding a grudge on my cold side of the bed.

"Tell me what's bothering you," he whispered. Now I felt trapped. If I said anything, we'd end up in a fight. If I didn't say anything, this would become one more thing I'd brush aside, adding to my list of resentments.

"I'm tired of being poor," I finally said. He stiffened, and I felt even more frustrated. Did he really think this would be a pleasant conversation? Was he surprised? I turned to face him. "I spent every penny I had on that doll. It hurt to spend that much all at once. I used what was left to buy cupcakes because I didn't have enough to buy an actual cake. But you show up like some knight in shining armor, and give her that car. How can I compete with that? It took me months to save for that doll. How could you afford something that extravagant?"

"I told you, it hardly cost me anything. It belonged to a friend, and we fixed it up."

"What friend?" I demanded. "As far as I can tell, your only friends in Oregon are the ones who live here, and none of them have kids. So what friend hooked you up with this brand new kids car?"

Instead of answering me, he sat up, slid to the edge of the bed, and picked up his shoes.

"I'm not listening to this bullshit," he said. "I go and do a nice thing for our daughter, and all you can do is yell at me."

"Stop trying to turn this on me! You didn't answer my question!"

"I don't need to answer your questions. I didn't do anything wrong. I'm tired of you acting like I'm some huge jerk, especially when I do something nice. It felt really good getting that car for Hope, and you're taking all the good feelings out of it."

"How do you think *I* feel?" I asked. "As soon as Hope saw that car, she dropped the doll in the dirt and forgot all about it. Everything I worked hard for was shoved aside when you showed up with that car. We could have had a better dinner tonight, and even for the rest of the week, for the money you probably spent."

"I told you! I got it from a friend!" He was standing now with clenched fists. I knew I should keep my mouth shut to avoid the inevitable. But my pride was stronger than my wisdom.

"Which friend, Jordan?"

He looked at me, then grinned and shook his head.

"You're unbelievable. You're just jealous my gift was better than some dumb doll you bought her. If it means that much to you, I'll tell Hope we both got her the car. I don't think she cares *who* it came from, but I'll let her know anyway."

"I don't want any part of your stupid gift," I said. "And I don't want any part of this stupid life. I'm so over this. You treat me like crap whenever we're together, we never have any money, this shack will only get colder when winter comes, and I don't want to live on a pot farm away from everyone I love."

"So you don't love me?" he asked.

"I didn't say that!"

"You just did. You said that you don't want to live away from everyone you love. So if that's true, then right now you don't live near anyone you love. That must mean you don't love Hope, either."

"That's not what I'm saying!" I yelled. His grin stayed on his face while I felt more frantic. I wanted to hit him where it hurt, to wipe that stupid grin off his face. I wanted to make him pay for every way he'd hurt me, shamed me, or made me feel alone. "I'm saying I gave up everything to move here because you made promises you couldn't keep. I was supposed to go to school, and I'm not. You said we could move out after six months, and we don't seem to have anything saved for that to happen. I'm tired of living this way, especially when I don't have to, and the next chance I get, Hope and I are out of here. I'm—"

I didn't get a chance to say anything else. He was on me, his hands at my throat as he straddled my body, his knees pulling the blankets taut against me. I couldn't move, and I grasped at his hands to keep him from choking me.

"Listen here, you bitch," he sneered. "If you leave me, I'll kill you. If you go back to Charlie, I'll kill him, too. I'll kill everyone you know in Petaluma, including that little boyfriend of yours. Don't think I don't know you fantasize about him. But he's a twig, and I'll snap him in two."

"You're hurting me!" I whimpered. He got closer to my face, and I turned my head to the side. I was tired of being his victim. "You can't stop me," I murmured. I looked back at him, narrowing my eyes as I mentally dared him to squeeze my neck harder. Maybe if I died, he'd be arrested. Then Hope wouldn't have to be around this monster.

He didn't squeeze harder. Instead, he reached back and slapped me across the face. I felt the sting all the way into my gut. Then he pulled me from the bed and threw me on the floor.

"Stop!" I screamed. He didn't. Instead, he kicked me in the stomach and I flew against the wall, vibrating the whole house as I curled up in a ball. He crouched down next to me, grabbing a chunk of my hair. I kept my head down, afraid to look at him.

"You think I can't stop you?" he hissed. "I don't give a fuck about you. You can go at any time. But if you take my daughter, I'll kill you. I'll kill anyone who tries to keep me from Hope. Try me, Maddie. See if I'm telling the truth."

He let go of my hair and stomped out of the room. I heard the door slam. I stayed on the floor, shaking as I cried. After a few minutes, I moved to my hands and knees and crawled to the living room to check on Hope. She'd slept through the whole fight.

I heard a knock and froze. It was near midnight. It couldn't be Jordan because he would have slammed his way in. The knock sounded again.

"Maddie?" I pulled myself to my feet.

"Hold on," I said, getting my robe. I pulled it on, then stopped in the bathroom. My face was red and blotchy with a purple mark forming where Jordan hit me. I closed my eyes and counted to ten. Then I went to the door and opened it a crack.

"Hey," I said.

"Hey," Ashton said back.

Forgive

"Are you okay?" Ashton asked. I nodded. He couldn't see me in the dim light through the crack in the door.

"I'm fine. We got in a little fight, that's all."

"That didn't sound like *a little fight*," he said. "Can I come in?"

Let him in? I could imagine what Jordan would do. I knew Ashton could hold his own, but I couldn't. That was obvious by how many times Jordan had broken me.

"I don't think that's a good idea," I told him. "Hope's still sleeping, and, well…"

"And Jordan will get mad," he finished. I nodded, opening the door slightly. "Did he do that?" He reached toward my cheek. I jerked away.

"It's nothing. It was an accident."

"Accidents don't look like that." He touched my face. I winced as the pain radiated, and put my hand on his and moved it away. He held my hand for a few seconds before I pulled back.

"Look, you shouldn't be here. I shouldn't be talking to you. You need to go."

He stared at me, then shook his head. "Why do you stay? What's in it for you?"

I couldn't answer. What *was* in it for me? *Nothing.* But I had nothing to go back to. I wasn't here by choice anymore; I was here because I ran out of choices. But I couldn't tell Ashton that; it would only open a door I wanted to keep closed.

"Because I love him," I lied.

"This isn't love."

"You don't know us!" I said. "You don't know what he's like, what I'm like, what our relationship's like. We had a fight. Every couple has fights. Yes, this one got a little out of hand, but he doesn't mean it. He takes care of us, and loves us. And I love him. And I think you need to leave."

He didn't move. I could see he wanted to say something, but he just gave me a sad smile.

"Fine. But if you're ever in trouble, come find me. I'm not afraid of your boyfriend."

I shut the door without saying goodbye, listening to his footsteps on the ramp.

But I am.

***

I woke to an empty bed in a freezing cold house. I turned the oven on to heat one side of the house, and the portable radiator on the other. By the time Hope and I sat at the table for breakfast, the house began to feel warm and Jordan breezed in through the door.

"It's getting cold out there," he said, tossing a bag on the futon.

"Daddy!" Hope said, climbing down from her seat so she could throw herself at his legs. I watched her hug him out of the corner of my eye, but refused to look at him. When I'd rechecked my appearance in the mirror this morning, my cheek was deep purple and there was a large bruise on my stomach. I hated being here. I should have left, except I believed him when he said he'd kill Charlie, Jace, and me if I ever tried—if I left with Hope, that is. And I wasn't about to leave without her.

Jordan set Hope down and came over to me. "Maddie."

I still wouldn't look at him, and I turned away. I knew I could be asking for another beating, but I was too hurt to speak to him. He sighed and he rustled through the bag on the bed.

"I got you something." I heard the hesitation in his voice, like he was afraid of my reaction. Good. I wanted him to suffer, beg for forgiveness, admit he was wrong. I knew the song and dance. We fight, he gets mad, I get mad, he silences me with his hands, I get hurt, he comes back and takes care of me. I knew what was going on. So why did I think this would ever end?

"It's getting cold," he repeated, placing a white jacket with fur lining over my shoulders. "I got you some gloves, too. And some for Hope. They match." When I looked up, his eyes were trained on my cheek.

"Thank you," I said, keeping all emotion from my face so he couldn't see me caving. I stood, still wearing the jacket, and started to clean the dishes.

"Wait," he said. *Here we go.* I knew his moves before he even made them. Worse, I knew my own. He came to me and cradled my face with his hand so he could get a good look at my cheek. Then he leaned in and kissed my cheek. I closed my eyes as he whispered apologies, touching his lips to my face every time he said he was sorry. Then he pulled me in. I resisted his embrace, remaining stiff, but relaxing as he continued to hold me. It was everything I needed. He'd hurt me. Now he was comforting me, and I needed that comfort more than I wanted to admit. The longer he held me, the more I wanted to melt into him, let him make me forget, accept his apology and pretend I believed he'd never do it again.

"You don't deserve someone like me," he told me, breaking our embrace at last. I knew it was the truth, and

I should just go with it and run. But as I looked in his eyes, I weakened. I needed reassurance.

"You told me you didn't want me," I said.

"It's not true."

"You told me you'd kill me if I took Hope from you." He looked embarrassed by these words.

"I don't want you to take Hope, and I don't want you to leave me."

"And you'll kill me if I do?"

"I was mad. I say things I don't mean when I'm mad."

"And you hit me when you're mad, too," I said.

"I won't do it again."

"I don't believe you. You've promised over and over this won't happen again, but you keep hurting me. What happens the next time I piss you off? What will stop you from hitting me?"

"I'll walk away," he said. I snorted through my nose. "No, really. I'll leave the house if I start to feel upset. Or if you see me getting upset, you can tell me to go cool off. I don't want to hurt you. I don't know why I do it. I need your help to stop. Will you help me?"

I looked down at my feet. I knew I was going to give in, and hated myself for it. I didn't know how to forgive him. I was sure I couldn't trust him. I looked at Hope playing with the doll, pretending they were having a tea party. What was I showing her by staying?

"Maddie?"

I looked at him. "Make me a promise," I said.

"Anything."

"We move from here before Christmas. I can't live here any longer. I need a real house and a real job. I want to go to school in the spring. Promise me all this will happen."

"I promise, babe. I'll make it happen. We *need* out of here."

My face softened into a smile, and he picked me up and swung me around the room. Hope saw this and wanted her turn, as well.

"Hey, let's get out of here. All three of us. What do you say?"

"In what car?" I asked, gesturing outside. He peered out the window at our car on cinder blocks.

"God, I'm kind of an asshole, aren't I?" I nodded, which made him laugh. "You're not supposed to agree with me!"

"When you take our only car apart because we had a fight..." I raised an eyebrow at him.

"All right, point taken. How about this? I'll go fix the car, and *then* we'll go do something as a family."

"How long will that take?" I asked.

"I just have to put the tires back on, and then we're good to go."

***

I watched from the window. Jordan got a couple guys to help out, and it only took half an hour. It was just long enough for Hope to fall asleep for her nap.

"I guess we can wake her," I said.

"Nah, she should sleep. Why don't we get someone to watch her?" he asked. I gave him a look.

"Right, because these guys are great at childcare since they guard pot plants."

"What about Eden?" he asked.

Eden and I never talked. I thought we'd become closer, but it never happened. However, she did step in for Hope when Jordan and I had that one fight in the courtyard. That moment alone qualified her for the job.

"You know she won't do it for free," I said. He nodded and pulled out a couple twenties. I stared at the money, then looked at him. "I thought you didn't have any money." I narrowed my eyes, daring him to lie.

"It just happened to be in my pocket," he promised. "Hand this to her and ask her to watch Hope for us."

I took the money and left the house. The closer I got to the warehouse, the more I second-guessed this decision. Eden would eat me for lunch just for believing she could babysit. What was I thinking?

Still, I went into the warehouse where she was reading on her cot in the corner.

"Hey," I said. She glanced at me, then went back at her book. I cleared my throat and touched her foot. "Hey," I said again. She put the book down with a sigh.

"What do *you* want?"

"Um, it's just that," I began. I collected myself and started over. "Uh, you remember that one time Jordan and I were in a fight and, uh..." I shook my head. "What I mean is—"

"Would you just spit it out?"

"Would you watch Hope for us?" I asked. Before she could say anything, I continued. "She's asleep right now, and probably will be for another hour or so. I'll make you guys sandwiches for lunch, and there's macaroni and cheese in the cabinet for dinner, if we're gone that long. She's not a bad kid, but you'll probably have to play tea party. You can stay at our house, and—"

"Okay," she said.

"Wait, really? You will?"

She got up and started putting her shoes on. "Yeah, I need to get out of this warehouse or I'll go crazy. Besides, I kind of like the little twerp. But once you're back, you have to let me take a shower at your place. The community bathroom is disgusting."

"Done!" I said. "You can even use my shampoo. It smells like strawberries."

"Don't get all girly on me. This is just me getting out of the warehouse and you going out for a night with that dipshit. We're not best friends or anything. And I want to be paid." I handed her two crumpled twenties. "Now we're in business."

Jordan and I left once Eden was set up in the house.

"Where are we going?" I asked.

"I thought we'd grab something to eat, and maybe head over to the lake, if you'd like. I stuck some fishing gear in the back."

We stopped at a café for burgers, fries, and sodas. When they served us, I was sure I couldn't eat the whole thing. Lately, we'd been eating light to keep our food budget small, and the burger was enough to feed me all day. I happily finished it, though.

Jordan drove us to a park near the lake. The day was surprisingly warm, and we lay on a blanket near the water. He set up the fishing poles, using bread as bait. It would be a long shot if we caught anything, but he'd prepared a cooler with ice from the café, just in case.

I took off my new jacket to feel the warm sun on my back, and Jordan did the same. We rested the fishing poles against rocks, and spent the afternoon talking. It was like old times, but better.

When we were younger, our conversations were shallow and self-focused. The only thing we had in common was how much we hated my parents' strict rules. We shared none of the same interests or views. He'd talk about stuff at the car shop; I'd tell him about school. Looking back, I couldn't see how our relationship got to the point of making a baby together, except that was the one thing we were good at.

Sitting next to a lake in Oregon, we now had a lot to say. Most of it was about Hope. We also told stories from our jobs on the farm, and gossiped about the people there. It was like nothing bad had ever happened in our relationship. Jordan felt like my friend, my partner.

"You're a good mom, you know that?" Even though we'd had a burger just a few hours before, we snacked on chips, throwing a few to some begging ducks.

"How so?"

He looked at me, squinting as the sun hit his face. "You just are. It comes so naturally to you. I watch you with her, and it's like you don't have to think about it. You make sure Hope has everything she needs, and put your own needs last."

"Thank you," I said. "I never feel like I'm doing anything special. I mean, I feel like I could be doing so much more. I should be working on teaching her letters to get her ready for preschool, or even just giving her more than I had when I was a kid."

"You do a lot," Jordan said. "Right from the beginning. You gave up your whole life to be her mother, even when you didn't have me around to help. She's so lucky to have you."

"Yeah, but I almost gave her away," I muttered. I wished the words back in as soon as I said them. I looked down at my hands as he reached over and took them.

"You wanted to give her a better life," he said. "Watching you with her now, I know you weren't trying to get rid of her. You love her too much, and you've sacrificed so much for her. I see how torn you must have been. I wish I'd been there for you. I wish I hadn't driven away. I wish I could have protected you instead of abandoning you."

His eyes filled with tears. I wiped one tear away as it escaped over his lashes. "You couldn't have, though. You were arrested."

"I know, but that was my fault. I shouldn't have stolen that money. If I'd found a job, none of this would have happened, and we would have been set." He touched my hand on his cheek, then squeezed it as he looked at me. "I don't deserve your love," he said. "That day you saw me in the coffee shop, you had every right to leave and never look back. But you forgave me. Why?"

Why did I forgive him? *Did* I forgive him? I was mad at him at first. But I lowered my guard because he was familiar, a link to my past. Most of all, he was Hope's father, and I wanted her to grow up knowing him. What better way than if the two of us were together?

"Everyone deserves another chance," I said. "I've made some pretty big mistakes, and I was given a second chance. You deserved the same kind of chance. Together, we made our beautiful little girl. Seeing you that day, I realized fate was giving the two of us a chance to be a family. It wasn't my place to stand in the way."

"Are you glad?"

I looked away, and he embraced me.

"I'm sorry things have been so rough lately," he whispered. "It's never about you. You're perfect."

"I'm far from perfect." My voice wavered.

"No, you really are," he said. "You take care of Hope and me, make sure everything is in order. You make the best of where we're living and the situation we're living in."

"But none of that's true," I said. "I complain all the time. I want off the farm; that's no secret. I scream at you and make threats about leaving."

"And I hurt you," he said. My tears blurred my vision. "I'm the one who's in the wrong. But you're still here with me. You still let me be Hope's daddy."

"Then why do you hurt me?" I asked, tears streaming down my cheeks.

"I don't want to. It just happens. It's like I black out or something. I think it's because I'm so frustrated here. It's not what I thought it would be. I know you're not happy, and I'm not, either. I'm stressed, I'm not sleeping enough, and when we fight, I can't think properly. We need to get out of here. But we can't yet."

"Can we at least start looking? Can I maybe get a different job? I bet I could qualify for some sort of aid to get Hope in daycare."

"Do you really want someone else to watch her?" Jordan asked.

"I don't see any other way. I want to earn a living, and I want to go to school. I can't have her with me at the same time."

"It can't happen right now." When I started to protest, he went on. "You made me promise we'd leave in December, and I'm not breaking that promise. That only leaves us two months. I need those months to set enough money aside and find a place for us to live. Plus, I have to find a way to tell Cody. He's already talking about plans for the next harvest, and I want to be gone before then."

"So, you'll really make it happen?"

"I promise." His lips pressed against mine, and I opened my lips to let him in. He tightened his embrace and kissed me more deeply. For the moment, I was able to forget everything bad in our relationship that made me unhappy. I was exactly where I wanted to be.

When we got back, Eden was building Lego castles with Hope. She rolled her eyes.

"If you tell anyone, you'll be sorry." Her expression softened. "I can't help it, I love Legos."

We let her take her shower, and invited her to stay for dinner. She said no, but told us she'd watch Hope again if we wanted to go out.

Once she left, I made us a spaghetti dinner with peas on the side. I mixed Hope's peas into her spaghetti, hoping she'd eat them that way. For the most part, it worked. The rest found their way to the floor. Jordan took over with Hope, cleaning her and getting her ready for bed while I waited for him in the bedroom. When he returned, I let him undress me, the anticipation building with each piece of clothing he removed. We made slow love that night, taking the time to touch each other, feel each other, and look into each other's eyes. Every time he pressed his mouth on mine, I rose up to reach him. We finished together, holding each other as the waves radiated throughout our bodies. I rolled on my side and curled into him so he was spooning me.

"Babe, I have to leave tonight," he whispered. I pulled away and faced him.

"Tonight? Really?"

"Really," he said. "I'm sorry, but they need me out at the plantation. It's my shift. I'm already late." He kissed my pout. "But maybe memories of tonight will keep us warm until I'm back."

"The real thing is better." I let him go, watching as he dressed. He kissed me again, this time on the forehead, and then left.

I wrapped myself deeper into the blankets. The bed was colder when he wasn't there. When I couldn't warm up, I put my sweats back on. I shivered for a little bit until I finally warmed up.

The day had been nice—the best we'd had since we'd been here. We spent all our time working or taking care of Hope, and we never paid enough attention to each other. Maybe that was all we needed. I started thinking of things we could do away from the farm. Sure, we'd have to pay Eden to watch Hope, but it was worth it to save our relationship.

9

Hungry

Six days. Six days and no Jordan. I'd tried calling him numerous times, but it always went straight to voicemail. I considered asking Cody, but then changed my mind. I'd stopped worrying, now I was mad. Six days he'd been gone, and there was almost no food left.

I gave Hope the last bowl of cereal for breakfast, and opened a can of beans for me. For lunch, there were still two slices of bread and peanut butter if I scraped from the sides of the jar. For dinner, I planned to make something out of the leftover beans and withered carrots in the fridge. I checked the car, but it was low on gas. I could make it into town, but I couldn't guarantee I could make it back. Even if I could, what would I do without money? I'd searched every corner of the house, hoping to find even a few coins. I found nothing. Jordan probably kept it on himself, which did me no good.

"Don't want this." Hope pushed away the dry cereal. I picked up the pieces that fell and put them back in the bowl.

"Then you can have it later, when you're hungry." I set the bowl on the counter.

"Mama, want pork chops."

I almost smiled, remembering the first time she asked for pork chops at Charlie's house. It felt so long ago. There were no pork chops then, either, so I fed her chicken and called them pork chops. Now, she was much too smart for that. There was no way she'd mistake a plate of beans or a bowl of cereal for pork chops.

"We don't have any pork chops," I told her, and she pouted. "But Daddy will get some next time he goes to the store."

The mention of pork chops made my stomach growl. I'd skipped dinner to make sure she ate, and that we'd have enough for today. I couldn't heat the beans fast enough. The stove was electric, and the burners took forever to get hot.

I heard a loud crack, and the lights went out. Swearing under my breath, I flipped the oven light switch. Nothing. The burners were cooling. My source of heat was gone.

I wanted to scream, to throw everything within my reach. I didn't ask for any of this. My stomach felt like it was ready to turn inside out, and it rumbled again. My chest tightened, and I wanted to cry. But when I looked at Hope, I knew I needed to pull myself together. She didn't ask for this, either. I couldn't afford to lose it.

I scraped a portion of the beans from the pot and put the rest in a container for later. I took a bite, then another. Once I got used to the temperature, it wasn't so bad.

Hope and I cuddled in her bed to keep warm while I read her stories. She nodded off after the third book, and I considered taking a nap. There wasn't anything else to do, after all. But I knew that was wrong. I could stop being a victim in this, and push back my pride. Just because Cody made me nervous didn't mean I should let us starve on account of it. He might even be able to bring Jordan in from the field.

I crept out of the bungalow to keep Hope from waking, and made my way to the warehouse. I had to force myself to put one foot in front of the other. My mind raced with all the things Cody could do to me without Jordan to protect me.

"Stop it, Maddie. Cody could have done any of these things all week long. He knows Jordan's not here."

Even still, I hesitated when I got to the warehouse. It was ridiculous, really. When Jordan and I first moved here, I wasn't this nervous. Now, I stayed in my house, refusing to come out. Jordan's abuse was one thing, but it was predictable. The unknown was much scarier. Worse, I knew Jordan would blame me if any of the guys touched me. Besides, with the vegetable garden dormant for the winter, I had no reason to come outside. Well, the sun maybe, but wasn't that what windows were for?

"Hey, girlie, haven't seen you around for a while. Want to join the card game?" I shook my head at the guy—his name was Ted, or Todd, or something like that. They were all watching me as I stood there, and I felt completely vulnerable.

"Um...is Eden here?" Maybe she'd let me borrow the money we gave her so we could get gas and food.

"She left a few days ago," I heard Cody say behind me. I turned around to face him, but looked down to avoid his gaze.

"What do you mean, *gone*?"

"We didn't need her anymore. She left early Tuesday."

"But she didn't even say goodbye!" This time I *did* look at him, regretting it as soon as he smirked at me.

"I didn't realize you two were friends."

We weren't. I knew that. But she'd watched my daughter. That was something, right? Or maybe it wasn't. Maybe I was reading more into this, as usual, because I was too stupid and naïve to see the truth.

"What do you want?" Cody asked.

"It's nothing." I turned to leave, but he caught me by the arm, letting go as soon as I pulled away.

"Tell me what it is, maybe I can help."

"Well, um, can you reach Jordan on the walkie-talkie? I need to talk with him."

"You can try, but the connection's really bad right now. They're probably out of batteries. Come with me."

My hands shook as I followed him toward his office. The memory of Bethany passed out on the couch haunted me. I wiped my sweaty hands on my pants when Cody handed me the radio.

I pushed the button to talk.

"Um, hello?" I said, my voice wavering. Cody laughed.

"It's not a phone. More than one person has a walkie on them. You have to say Jordan's name so he knows to pick up. Here, like this." He took it from me, and placed it to his mouth. "J-bird, do you copy?" He waited. We heard static around Jordan's voice. I couldn't make out what he was saying, though. "Repeat that, over," Cody said. Again, static and garbled words. He looked at me and shrugged, and moved to turn off the radio.

"You need to call him in," I insisted.

"I don't *need* to do anything," Cody said, raising an eyebrow at me.

"It's important. Please, I'll do anything." He moved toward me, and I backed up a step.

"If you're willing to do anything, I'll take you there myself."

"That's not what I mean." I looked around the room for something to use in defense.

"Then you must not need him that badly." He inched closer to me.

"Forget I said anything. I'll leave you alone." He grabbed me and I struggled to get free. It was just like the day Jordan's dad had attacked me, but he'd been drunk and clumsy, and Cody was sober and strong. He pinned me on the couch with his legs and pulled at my pants as I tried to kick at him. Nothing worked, and I panicked, trying to shove him off me. I screamed, unwilling to go down without a fight.

"Shut your mouth, you bitch," he growled, smothering my cries with his hand. I bit him, tasting the coppery blood in my mouth, and he pulled back, swearing. His eyes burned as he reached back, and I prepared for him to hit me.

"Get off her!"

I felt Cody yanked from me, and saw Ashton shoving him against the wall.

"What do you think you're doing, man?"

"Dude, she asked for it. You should have seen it. It's like she doesn't even know she has a boyfriend."

"Are you okay?" Ashton pulled me off the couch. I looked at them, then ran all the way to the bungalow. Hope was still asleep as I locked the door. Even that didn't feel safe. Cody probably had a key to the place. I looked around for something to put in front of the door. The table didn't look big enough, but the mattress might be. I was pulling it off the bed when there was a knock. I froze as the knocking continued.

"Go away!"

"It's me, Ashton." I paused, unsure what to do. I never should have left. I didn't need this kind of trouble.

"What do you want?"

"To help you," he said. "Please open the door."

I took a deep breath, placing my hand against the door as I contemplated my actions. I could refuse to open the door and maybe he'd go away. Or I could open it and let him in.

"Maddie, please."

I inched the door open, peering out at his concerned face.

"I'm not your enemy," he said.

I looked at my feet, and nodded. "I know. I was just..."

"You were scared. Can I come in?"

"I don't know."

"Just for a few minutes. You're letting all the heat out."

"There's no heat," I told him. "The power went out this morning. I can't turn on the heater or lights. I can't even cook anything, not that there's anything to cook."

"You don't have any food?" Before I could say anything, he pushed his way into the house and went to the kitchen.

"Come on in," I muttered. "It's not like I get any say around here."

He ignored me and opened the refrigerator. I looked away as he stared at the empty shelves. We didn't even have butter.

"You're coming with me," he said, shutting the fridge.

"But Hope is sleeping," I said.

"Then wake her. We're going out."

"Ashton, you know I can't."

"Do you think Jordan would want you to starve?" he asked. "He'd want his daughter to eat, I'm sure. Grab your stuff, let's go. We can take your car."

"We have no gas," I whispered, embarrassed.

"Then we'll put gas in it. Let's go."

***

After filling the tank, Ashton drove us to a restaurant. Despite my growling stomach, I asked him to find one out of town. I didn't want anyone who knew Jordan or Ashton to see us and think the wrong thing. I knew it was unlikely, but I didn't want to take any chances. It was bad enough I'd agreed to this. I already felt guilt washing over me, Jordan's names for me echoing in my head. *Slut. Whore. Cheater. Liar.*

But I'm not, I told myself. This was necessary. If we didn't eat, we starved. Besides, this was more for Hope than for me.

At the diner, Ashton told me to order whatever I wanted. I didn't want to spend all his money, so I asked for a grilled cheese and soup for me, and a quesadilla for Hope. When it was Ashton's turn, he ordered a burger and several appetizers. We waited in awkward silence after I shut down some of Ashton's questions about my life.

"I'm not in the mood for talking," I said. It felt mean, especially when he was going out of his way for us. If I hurt his feelings, he didn't tell me.

The waitress came back with nachos, bread, and crab dip. I tried not to be greedy, but after the first bite of nachos, I realized how hungry I was.

"Just eat," Ashton said, watching as I tried to be polite. He demonstrated by taking several chips off the plate and stuffing them in his face. Then he put some on a plate in front of Hope, and she happily began to eat. I brushed aside my manners and went for it, each bite chopping away at my hunger.

Our lunch came, and I stared longingly at Ashton's burger as my soup steamed in front of me. I was glad he'd gotten appetizers, because this never would have held me over.

"Here." Ashton put half of his burger on my plate.

"But you'll be hungry!" I said.

"If I am, I'll get more food. You need to eat."

I stopped arguing, and took a big bite. It was even better than the burgers Jordan and I had eaten the week before.

Halfway through my meal, I finally felt normal— comfortable enough to look at him, even speak. He asked about Hope, my parents, and where I lived before. I didn't mention the shameful parts, just gave generic answers. I turned the conversation back to him, and he told me that his dad and Cody's were brothers, and his mom was Creole, explaining their different skin color. He'd live in Louisiana, but wanted a change, and Cody offered him a job.

"You don't mind that it's…" I trailed off, feeling dumb for not being able to say it in public.

"Marijuana?" he asked.

"Well, yeah," I said. "Or do you smoke it, too?"

"Occasionally," he admitted. "Look, I'm no angel. But I'm not a pothead, either. I smoke now and then to unwind a little. Have you ever smoked?"

I shook my head, moving my gaze to the table.

"Never? Whoa. So this is kind of a culture shock, isn't it?"

"You could say that. I didn't know what we were getting into when Jordan brought us here. I thought it was a regular farm."

"So he tricked you."

"Well, no. I mean, sort of. I had a feeling about it, but he didn't come out and say it until I asked. I should have known, though." I felt my cheeks flush. I was way out of my league. To everyone at the farm, this was normal life. To me, this was the kind of stuff you read about in the news, usually when someone was arrested.

"Why are you even here?" His question caught me off guard. I looked at him for a moment, wondering if he was joking.

"Because you brought me here," I told him.

"No, I mean, why are you on the farm? Why are you here with Jordan? What are you getting out of this?"

It was the same conversation as the week before. I started to answer, but he cut me off.

"Don't tell me you love him," he said. "I don't believe it."

"I do!" I glanced at Hope to see if she was listening; she was still eating, not even paying us any attention. "This is temporary. I probably shouldn't tell you this, since Jordan hasn't told Cody yet, but we're leaving in December. We're getting our own place and regular jobs. Then we're saving up for our own farm—a legal one."

"This one's legal," Ashton said with a wink. I raised my eyebrow at him. "Okay, fine. It would be legal if Cody bought the land he's growing on and get the proper permits. But he's never been one to follow the rules." He took another bite of food, and then gave me a long look. "So you're leaving in two months?"

"Yup."

He nodded. "It's funny, because Cody was making plans for next year, and Jordan's name is all over it."

"I told you, Cody doesn't know we're leaving."

"Yeah, but still, it seems strange that Jordan would give up something like this when Cody's paying him so well."

"He is?" I had no idea how much money Jordan made. Now that I wasn't making anything, I relied on what he gave me, which was close to nothing since I had no reason to have any money.

"He's one of the top dogs here, though I don't know why. The guy blows so much smoke; it's insane that anyone believes a word he says." He glanced at me. "Um, I mean…"

"No, it's okay," I said. "I get it. And I'm one of those dummies who thinks his word is gospel."

"I didn't mean it that way."

"I know." I stared at my half-eaten soup, stirring it to find a few pieces of chicken at the bottom. "What you said is true. As long as I've known Jordan, he's always had an answer for everything. He's talked me into so many things, and I follow him blindly, forgetting the destruction he always leads us into. Not one thing he's suggested has turned out well." I fumed as I thought back to the day he talked me into stealing a woman's wallet when we arrived in Petaluma. Why did I keep trusting him? Why *now*, especially? How could I let him talk me into leaving Charlie's home for something unknown? Looking at our history together, did I really think things would be different?

"Oh my God, I'm the definition of insanity," I whispered.

"What?"

"Insanity. Doing the same thing over and over and expecting different results. I keep doing this, believing Jordan when he says he has a plan, and tells me to trust him. What *am* I doing?"

"That's what I just asked you," Ashton said with a chuckle. He took my hand to comfort me, but I pulled away, looking at Hope to see if she noticed. She was playing with her food on the table, but turned to me when she became aware I was watching her.

"All done," she said.

"Okay, but hang tight. We're almost finished." Ashton waved down the waitress for our bill. I couldn't look while he paid, feeling terrible that I couldn't contribute a few dollars. As we were leaving, I whispered my thanks.

"It's nothing." He kept his distance while we walked, or maybe it was me keeping *my* distance.

I protested when we pulled into the parking lot of a grocery store.

"How am I supposed to explain this to Jordan?" I asked. "What do I say when he sees food he didn't buy in our refrigerator?"

"You tell him you were starving and desperate, so I bought you food," Ashton said. I sank in my seat, knowing that would send Jordan over the edge. Still, I couldn't stand the thought of going home to no food.

"I can't have you keep doing stuff for us," I protested.

"You haven't asked me to do one thing, even though I keep telling you I can help. I'm doing this on my own. You just happen to be along for the ride."

We walked the aisles of the grocery store. He told me to start loading the cart with things I needed, but I couldn't bring myself to do it. We passed milk, eggs, cheese, and our cart remained empty.

"You know, I'm just going to start putting stuff in here," Ashton said. "If you disagree, you can take it out."

I wrinkled my nose, but didn't stop him. He was right as many times as he was wrong. After putting the seventh wrong item back on the shelf, it started to feel like a game. We sped things up, and even Hope was laughing as we moved down the aisles collecting food. When we were done, the cart was packed, and my guilt was overwhelming. The game was over, and reality set in.

"We have to put most of this back."

"Nope. You accepted all those items." He headed toward the register, but stopped when he saw I wasn't following. "Maddie, why does everything have to be so difficult with you?"

I avoided his gaze, remembering another time someone had bought me groceries. It felt like history was repeating itself. Jordan's dad had taken me out to eat. Then he bought groceries for all of us. After, he came to my room, expecting me to put out. In his mind, he'd done something nice for me, so he expected me to do something "nice" for him.

Did Ashton expect the same thing?

"We have to put it all back," I insisted, pulling Hope from the cart. "I don't want any of it."

"Maddie..."

I walked out of the store. The car was locked, so I leaned against it, shifting Hope so she faced me. She played with my hair and flirted with me, trying to get me to smile. I did, pretending everything was fine. Inside, I worried. What had I done? I'd let Ashton buy our lunch. I let him buy our groceries.

"How could I be so stupid?" I whispered.

"You not stupid," Hope told me, placing her little hand on my cheek. Her hands were cold from the frigid air.

"I know, baby. I'm just kidding," I told her, taking her hand and blowing my warm breath on it.

"This one," she said when I was done, placing her other cold hand on my mouth. As I blew, all I could think of was how I'd led Ashton on up to this point. He'd probably call me a tease. I probably was. Who did anything for anyone these days without expecting something in return? I wasn't so special that people were falling over themselves to do things for me. He'd expect payment. The question was, how much?

Ashton came out fifteen minutes later, pushing a grocery cart full of bags. I knew he would. Why else was he taking so long? Still, I turned my back and wouldn't look as he approached the car.

"Hey," he said when he reached us. "What happened in there?"

"Nothing," I mumbled. I knew I had to help him put the bags in the car. He'd already bought them. But I'd be damned if I actually took them.

We loaded the trunk and placed a few bags next to Hope, as well. Then we made the drive back to Eugene. I watched the scenery, trying to figure out how to ask what he wanted from me. Maybe if I left the groceries in the car, he'd get the hint and keep them for himself.

"Maddie, talk to me."

I gathered my courage. I wanted those groceries. The thought of eating the rest of the beans from this morning, or going to bed hungry one more night was too much. But I would not have sex with him.

"I'm not having sex with you." As I said it, I wished I could stuff the words back in my mouth. There were a million better ways I could have started that conversation.

"I didn't realize that was on the table," he said, his eyes laughing.

"I'm serious! I don't know what you were thinking when you bought us lunch and all that food, but I can't have sex with you. If that's a deal breaker, keep your groceries."

Ashton didn't say anything right away. Instead, he pulled the car off the road and parked. Then he turned to me. I leaned against the door, unsure what he was doing. He seemed angry, but as soon as he looked me over, his expression softened.

"I want to punch every single person who made you believe this way," he said. I didn't say anything, but felt my body relaxing in my seat. "You're a pretty girl. Guys must fall all over themselves when it comes to you. But I'm not after you. I don't want anything from you, except for you and your daughter to be safe and fed."

"But that was a lot of money," I argued.

"And so you're supposed to have sex with me to get it?" he asked. I looked away. "Have I given you any reason to think I'm that kind of guy?"

"No," I said, continuing to stare out the window.

"I did it because you were hungry, and because you have a little girl who needs food more than both of us."

"But it's so much!" I cried. I glanced in the back seat. Hope was playing with a toy we'd left in the car, ignoring us.

"It's my money," he said. "And I have enough." He studied me for a moment, then sighed. "Look. I had a hard life growing up. It seemed like we were always poor. I never understood those people who called a full refrigerator empty. Our fridge really was bare. There were nights my mom went hungry so we could eat. We had a farm next to us, and I stole eggs and produce so we could eat. I almost got shot a couple of times. I remember having to go to bed hearing my little brothers crying because they were still hungry. There was nothing we could do. When we were between paychecks and the money ran out, we could only wait until the next payday. I used to fantasize about some person coming into our home, seeing how we were living, and taking pity on us. Kind of like a fairy godmother, you know? So when I opened your refrigerator, it reminded me of when I had nothing, and no one showed up to help us out. I didn't want you to have to experience the same thing."

"I've experienced worse," I said. "We'd have survived."

"*You* would have, but would Hope? Would you really have been okay with her crying herself to sleep hungry?"

I shook my head, staring at my lap.

"Then let me buy these for you. If there's any kind of payment, it's in letting me turn a bad memory into a good one. I want to help you. I *need* to help you."

I looked into his eyes and saw the sincerity. I lowered my shoulders, which I hadn't realized I was holding up close to my ears, and offered him a smile.

"Thank you."

"Now, was that so hard? Sheesh."

***

Back at the farm, Ashton helped me carry the groceries into the house. I saw the guys in the warehouse watching us, and knew they'd tell Jordan. I was starting to not care. He'd let us go hungry, and another man had to buy us food. This was his fault, not mine. Now I had to convince him of that.

We still had no power, so Ashton checked the breaker box I hadn't known was on the other side of the house. A few clicks of the switches and the lights were back on. I turned on the heater and we put the food away. He didn't stick around after that. I think he knew it was better on my end if he didn't. I felt bad, like I still owed him something for the food—at least an hour or two to hang out. But he meant it when he said no payment was necessary. So when he left, I locked the door, then turned to Hope.

"What should we make for dinner? We have a gazillion choices!" I wasn't really hungry after the huge lunch, but the novelty of having so much food made me want to cook a bunch of it.

She tilted her head to the side.

"Pork chops?"

"I believe I can do that," I laughed, went to the kitchen, and opened the fridge.

***

Jordan came back the next day. Hope was asleep and I was lying down to take a nap when I heard him come in. I held my breath as I heard his footsteps go to the kitchen and the sound of the refrigerator opening. I could picture him standing in front of it, wondering how it got there. I didn't move. I heard him rummaging around the shelves, and then the refrigerator door closed. He opened and closed drawers, and put things on the sink. When I heard his footsteps again, I closed my eyes and stayed still. I knew he was watching me. When I couldn't handle it any more, I opened my eyes. He was leaning against the doorjamb, eating a sandwich.

"Hey." I didn't know what else to say.

"Hey. Where did the food come from?"

"Where have you been for a week?" I asked, ignoring his question.

"At work. Where did the food come from?"

"And did you know you'd be working for a week?" I asked.

"Maybe," he answered. "Now, the food?"

"And did you realize when you left that night to be gone for a week, you left us without any food or money?"

"There was food. Stop being so dramatic."

"No, there wasn't. The night you left, we were due for a grocery-shopping trip. If you'd been gone for one night, like usual, it wouldn't have been a big deal. But we ran out of food yesterday. We would have run out sooner, but I rationed the food we had. When we did run out, I had to do something."

"Where did the food come from?" he repeated.

I sat up, bracing myself for what would happen next.

"Ashton."

I saw his face darken.

"So you went calling on your little boyfriend instead of coming to get me," he said, taking a step toward me.

"I tried to get you!" I insisted. "I called you on the walkie-talkie, but I couldn't get through."

"Then you could have had one of the guys come out to get me."

"I'm not having any of them do anything for me," I hissed. He raised an eyebrow at me. Then he smiled.

"Except for Ashton, right? You won't have anyone come out to get me, but you'll take free handouts from him. Or, *were* they free?"

"You don't know anything," I said, narrowing my eyes as I stood up. He stayed put, watching me. "We were on our last food yesterday. It was a can of beans, cereal, and two pieces of bread. That was it. I know you don't want me talking to anyone when you're not here. But if I didn't, we'd starve. So I went to Cody to see if he could reach you. When we couldn't, Cody decided I *did* owe him something, and he tried to rape me."

Jordan's expression changed at this. "He what?" he asked.

"You heard me. He tried to rape me, like he raped Bethany. But Ashton stopped him, and you have *him* to thank that I wasn't raped yesterday. You also have him to thank for all the food in our house. When he saw that you'd left your daughter and me here without anything to eat, he insisted on getting us food."

"What was he doing in our house?"

"He was helping me after Cody attacked me!"

"And what did he want in return?" Jordan asked.

"Nothing! He did it to be nice. Is that so hard to believe, that people might do something nice for someone else?"

"It is in my world," he muttered. He took another bite. When he was done chewing, he sighed and shook his head.

"What?" I asked.

"Now I'll owe that prick for giving us food," he said.

"No, you're not," I said. "He said there were no strings attached."

"Not for you, at least," Jordan said. "He's going to hold this over me for a long time."

"Not that long," I told him. "We're moving in December, remember?"

He nodded.

"Are you even concerned that your boss attacked me while you were gone?" I asked him.

"Of course I'm concerned," Jordan said. "But I also told you those guys are no good. That's why I want you to stay away from them."

"Then make sure you always leave us with enough."

10

Twenty

Jordan made sure we never went hungry again. It took a while to get used to a full refrigerator and cabinets. The first few weeks, I celebrated each shopping trip with an elaborate dinner, making up for our dull life by being creative with our food. After a while, even this got old—especially when Jordan was never there to enjoy it.

His frequent absences began gradually. At first, it was just a day or two. Work had slowed down on the farm as the temperature dropped, so I knew he wasn't spending time in the field. He didn't deny this. He was finding work for both of us, he told me, and was looking for a new place to live.

This was all I wanted. It was a sign he was following through and we'd finally be free of this hellhole. However, when weeks had gone by and there was still nothing, I began to wonder what was going on—especially when his absences became longer and more frequent. It wasn't even that he was gone, it was that he was unreachable. I'd call, and get no answer. I'd text…nothing. I'd even try to track him with the location service on my phone, feeling like a stalker, but it seemed like he'd hidden his location on his phone. I was afraid to ask him about it, knowing it would only out me for trying to keep tabs on him.

We fought—or didn't talk—when he was home. Or we had sex, only for him to leave soon after. We were two separate beings floating around the same space, our only connection being Hope. She was oblivious to it all, as she should have been. We were her two favorite people. When I was there, she clung to me, wanting me to entertain her in our prison-like home. When Jordan was there, she was all over him. It was the only time I saw him smile—a *real* smile, that is. He always lit up when he saw her. But when he looked at me, nothing. I couldn't read him. It was like I didn't know him anymore. He didn't touch me when we talked, or even acknowledge me if he didn't have to. I didn't think he even loved me anymore. But Hope? He was devoted to her.

This was the only thing keeping me from leaving. No, that wasn't true. There were many things keeping me from leaving. He took the car when he left, leaving me with no transportation. Even if I could leave, I wouldn't know where to go. The door to my cage was open, but my safety existed within these four walls. I had no money, no friends, and no one to turn to. The world out there was the big unknown, and I'd never survive in it. It didn't matter that I'd done it before, this time there was more at stake—I had Hope. That alone made this bungalow shack, the very space where Jordan lashed out at me, safe.

Besides, it had been a while since Jordan had attacked me. We still argued. He still threatened my life, or Charlie's, and even Jace's, on occasion. When he'd accuse me of cheating, I'd throw it right back at him, asking who he was screwing since he was always on my case about it. I told him he was worthless, getting right up in his face as if daring him to hit me. In truth, I *was* goading him, waiting to see if he'd lay his hands on me so I'd have more reason to hate him. But he didn't. I don't know why, but it made me even madder. It was almost like he was saying I was no longer worth getting that angry about. He didn't love me enough to get angry. Therefore, he didn't hit me. Sometimes he'd walk out, just like he told me he would. But it wasn't about having the last word; it was about ending his sentence and slamming the door on mine.

***

I woke up on the morning of my birthday while it was still dark outside. Jordan's side of the bed was empty, as it had been the past two nights. I was getting used to his absences. If I hadn't been stuck here, I would have enjoyed him being gone. It meant I could move around the house freely without feeling like an intruder. It meant Hope wanted to be around me. But it also meant I couldn't leave the house. The door lock was flimsy. Still, I pretended the locks meant something, and refused to go outside and invite trouble.

Hope was asleep when I tiptoed through the living room and into the kitchen. I made a cup of tea and leaned into the fragrant steam. Then I crept outside and shut the door behind me.

There was a light dusting of snow. It probably wouldn't snow any more than this, but the cold made it feel like a blizzard was coming. I felt alone, making the scene in front of me feel like a muted version of itself, the colors pink from the just-rising sun. If I hadn't known any better, I would have been awed by the early morning's beauty. I would be delighted in the silence, interrupted occasionally by a few brave birds. I'd be planning our winter fun, thinking about snowball fights and hot chocolate, and looking forward to Christmas. I'd know that today was the best day, because it was my birthday, and everybody has a good day on their birthday.

But I knew better.

I walked down the ramp, pulling my jacket tighter to my chest as I found a nearby rock. Sitting down, I looked out at the farm, drinking in the scene with each sip of tea, thinking about the past few years and how I came to be here.

What are you doing, Maddie?

I thought back to the day my parents kicked me out of their home. I'd told them I was pregnant. I knew they'd be mad, especially my dad. I thought he might take it out on Jordan, which was why I decided to tell them on my own. I hadn't expected my dad to tell me to leave, though. At first I'd thought it was a joke, or something he was saying to make himself feel better. But when he gave me a time limit of just a few minutes to get out of their house, I realized he was serious. I was Jordan's problem now, he told me. When he slammed the door behind me, I was left to figure out life on my own.

"And here I am now," I whispered. This wasn't my parents' fault. I wanted to blame them for this and every other bad thing that had happened to me. They deserved my blame. When I needed them most, they turned their backs on me. I wasn't prepared to take care of myself, let alone become a mother. However, where I was now had nothing to do with them. This was *my* doing. I couldn't even blame Jordan. I believed him when I shouldn't have. When he left me at that grocery store to take the rap for a crime we planned together, that should have been the end of it. I'd endured months of homelessness before Charlie and Viola took me in. With their help, I'd created a good environment for Hope to grow up in. I was planning my future. I was on my way to freedom. And then I threw it all away when Jordan showed up. I knew better! His track record had already proven I'd be disappointed by him. Still, I believed him, giving up everything stable so we could be a family.

"Is this the family you were hoping for?" I whispered, watching the rays from the morning sun settle on the glistening snow, slowly melting it away. I'd had a family; I just hadn't fully accepted it. If Charlie could see what was happening now, he'd be beside himself. Maybe he was still hurt over what I'd said to him. He might be mad that I left without saying goodbye, or that the car he gave me was now an ugly primer gray and driven primarily by Jordan. He'd be furious that I brought Hope with me to live on a pot farm. But he loved us. All this time I'd told myself he'd never take us back. If he'd been like my biological father, that would have be true. But Charlie didn't work that way. If I went home, he'd welcome me back.

Do I deserve his forgiveness?

"Whatcha thinking about?"

Ashton stood in front of me. I started to get up to leave, but he held his hands up.

"Don't go. I thought you could use company." He sat down on the rock next to me, and it took everything I had not to bolt. I hadn't seen him since the day he put food in my refrigerator. I still felt like I owed him something. What he'd done had been so nice. And I'd repaid him by becoming a hermit.

"Hope will wake up soon."

"She'll wake up? Or you don't want to be near me?" he asked. I studied my tea, now cold from the winter air. When I didn't answer, he nudged my shoulder. "It's all right. I get it."

We sat there for a good twenty minutes, saying nothing. Not on the outside. Inside, my thoughts were loud. I couldn't help wondering *what* he got. Why did he think I wasn't coming outside anymore? What was he doing here? What did he want? What if Jordan came home? Should I leave him here? Do I stay?

He got up, finally, and I let out a breath I didn't even know I was holding.

"Good seeing you, Maddie. I hope we can do this again." As he turned away, I realized this was probably the most conversation I'd have all day. I didn't know when Jordan was coming home. I doubted he remembered my birthday. I hadn't reminded him, knowing it would feel more special if he remembered on his own. But now, it felt like a stupid idea. If he forgot, which he probably would, it would make this day worse.

"It's my birthday." Ashton turned as I wondered what I was thinking.

"Why didn't you say so?" he asked. "What do you guys have planned?"

"Nothing. I mean, he might surprise me. It's not a big birthday or anything. I'm only twenty."

"You're twenty? That's kind of a big deal. You're not a teenager anymore."

"Yeah, but I can't go get a drink or run for president. It's just a regular, nothing special birthday."

He studied me. I couldn't tell what he was thinking. Then he slowly nodded his head. "Well, I hope your birthday is truly special. Happy birthday."

"Thanks." I watched him walk back to the warehouse. I felt stupid. *What did I want—a prize for turning a year older?*

***

Hope and I spent the day inside, as usual. I made pancakes for breakfast, breaking into the sausage in the freezer so we could eat Pigs in a Blanket. Then we created a small town with her blocks. For lunch, we split a can of soup and had grilled cheese sandwiches. She went down for a nap, and I stared out the window for an hour. By the time I was tired enough to lie down for a nap, she was up again.

It felt like any other day, and I was restless. So when I heard a knock on the door, I forgot my fear and bounded to the door. Ashton stood there, holding a bunch of balloons in one hand, and balancing a bag and a small gift on top of a pink dessert box in the other.

"It's not much," he said. "But it was short notice."

I wanted to laugh at how his idea of a small gesture was so huge, and spin in circles over his thoughtfulness. Instead, I burst into tears.

"Hey," he said, walking in without an invitation. He released the balloons and set down everything he was carrying. Untethered, the balloons floated to the ceiling, their strings hanging like jungle vines. Then he gave me a hug.

I hated that I couldn't stop crying. I didn't need him to see this weak side of me. But today had been such a bust. It was near dinner, and Jordan hadn't shown up. I didn't even know what his presence would do. If he never came home, my day would be ruined. But if he came home and had forgotten it was my birthday, everything would be worse. And here I was, in my living room, hugging a boy who wasn't my boyfriend. This made me cry harder, which made Ashton hold me tighter.

"Mama, you crying?" Hope asked. I pushed Ashton away and wiped my face.

"Yes, sweetie. But I'm okay now," I said, trying to smile through the tears. I turned to Ashton. "I'm sorry. You shouldn't be here."

The look on his face made me feel terrible for saying it. He'd done more for me than my own boyfriend. But that was why he needed to go. He was confusing me.

"I'll pretend you didn't say that," Ashton said, then turned around and opened the bag. "Hope, do you like tacos?"

"Yes!" she squealed, and sat down on the floor with the taco he handed her. Cheese and meat fell on the floor, and she ate what was in her hand before working on what she dropped.

I crunched into the taco Ashton gave me, fighting back more tears as I did.

"Tell me what you're thinking," he whispered. I shook my head as my eyes spilled over. I turned my back to him, continuing to eat the taco even though I could hardly taste it. He touched my back, and I flinched, which only made me cry harder. "Turn around," he said. I shook my head. I felt his hands on my shoulders and he moved me so I was facing him. I kept my eyes focused on my knees. "No one should be alone on their birthday," Ashton said. I couldn't look at him. "And what Jordan is doing is fucked up."

"Ashton, please," I said, glancing at Hope.

"No, you, *please*. This has to stop. You let him treat you like crap, dismiss you, throw you around, and then disappear for days at a time. You're worth so much more than this. You deserve to be thought of first."

"You don't know me," I told him. "You don't know what goes on in this house."

"I know enough. Tell me I'm not telling the truth."

I looked away. "And I suppose you're here to rescue me," I muttered. He reached over and put his finger under my chin, gently guiding me so that I was facing him.

"No," he said. "I'm trying to get you to rescue yourself."

"There's nothing to—"

"Bullshit."

I glared at him; at the nerve he had to sit here in *my* house, in front of *my* daughter, while he badmouthed her father and implied I should leave. I was furious with him for even suggesting any of it. I was even angrier that he was right. I wiped my hands on my jeans, and took a deep breath.

"I've forgotten how."

"You just need to leave."

"I know, but I don't know how." When he started to speak, I cut him off. "I know, I get in the car and drive away. Then what? Where do I go? What do I do? How do I survive?"

"How are you surviving *here*?" he asked.

"Because Jordan gives us everything. He works and makes the money. He gets our food. He takes care of everything. Without him, I have nothing."

"And soon, he'll have nothing, too," Ashton said. "Cody's decided that Jordan's overstayed his welcome." I started at this, feeling the anger well up inside me.

"Because of the day Cody tried to attack me," I spat out.

"I don't know," Ashton said, and I narrowed my eyes. "Okay, fine. It probably has plenty to do with it. But there's more to it than that. He and Jordan haven't been agreeing lately. But Cody hasn't kicked him out yet because of you and Hope—"

"How generous of him."

"I know. Cody's a prick for what he did. But he doesn't want to see you and your daughter out in the cold."

"Right, and he'll probably invite us to stay in his room to keep us safe."

Ashton sighed. "The bottom line is, Jordan's time is almost up. Cody plans to can him by the end of the week, and that means you all lose your home."

"Well, that's fine. Jordan's been looking for a place for us to move," I told him. Ashton shook his head. "What do you know?" I asked.

"That Jordan's been pissing away the money," he said. "Jordan talks a lot of smack. And he brags a lot, too. He went on and on about how he bought Hope that motorized car. It cost him $500, money he won gambling at the casino. He keeps going back there, trying to win more. A few weeks ago, though, he got wasted and admitted that he was almost out of money. He's been trying to win it back, but hasn't yet."

"But he was looking for jobs for us," I insisted. "And he bought all this food."

"I don't know what to tell you."

I felt like I'd been kicked in the gut. How could Jordan do this? He'd promised we'd get out of here, and his solution was to lose all our money at the casino. Now we had to leave, with nowhere to go.

"Do you understand, now?" Ashton asked. "You need to get out of here before the shit hits the fan. You don't need to be a part of this kind of life. It's not doing anything for you, and this is no place to raise your daughter."

"But I still don't know where to go," I told him.

"I'm sure you know someone," he said. I closed my eyes. I did. But would he take me back? I opened my eyes, and I gave a small nod. "Look, I know this is scary for you," he said. "I want to help any way I can. You just let me know when the light is green, and I'll take care of things on this side."

"How?" I asked him. "Are you going to hurt him?"

"No, nothing like that. But I'll do my best to give you the head start you need." Ashton stood, grabbing the dessert box and the package off the counter. "For now, let's celebrate. It's not every day you turn twenty."

"You shouldn't have," I said as he opened the box. Inside were three cupcakes. I noticed there was none for Jordan. Hope clapped her hands as Ashton gave her a cupcake. Then he handed one to me.

"I draw the line at singing, so I hope you don't mind not getting a birthday song today," he said.

"You've done more than enough," I told him.

"Don't forget this," he said, placing the gift in my lap. I set the cupcake on the floor and picked up the package. I slid the lid off the box. Inside was a small gold chain bracelet with a gold butterfly on it. There was a small crystal on one of the butterfly's wings.

"It's beautiful," I told him, giving him a hug.

"What kind of fuckery is this?" I heard Jordan say from the doorway.

11

Shattered

Jordan strode past me and grabbed Ashton by the shirt. Ashton was ready for it, though, and managed to push Jordan off him before scrambling to his feet.

"Daddy!" Hope whimpered, and I crawled over and pulled her to me, scooting us between the wall and the couch, trying to make myself small.

"I'm gone for a few days and you're swooping in on my girl?" Jordan yelled.

"I'm not swooping in on anyone's girl," Ashton said. "It's her birthday, or did you forget?"

"I don't care what day it is, get the fuck out of my house."

"Look bro—"

"I ain't your bro, Ashton." Jordan squared his shoulders, his eyes full of anger. He turned in my direction. "I was right about you all along, Maddie. You're just some filthy whore who's using me. Why don't you go back to your daddy? Oh yeah, I forgot. He doesn't want you, just like no one around here wants you."

"Don't talk to her that way." Ashton pushed Jordan so that he stumbled backward. When he caught his footing, he came at Ashton again. Ashton grabbed him and threw him face down on the ground, pinning his arm behind him and pressing his knee into Jordan's back. "You listen here, buddy, and listen good. This has gone on long enough. You leave your girlfriend and your daughter alone here for days at a time, even knowing that Cody attacked Maddie, and he'll do it again if he thinks he can get away with it. I've been protecting your girl while you're away, making sure Cody leaves her alone. Where are you while all this is going on? What is so important that you can't be here to protect her? Maddie's done nothing wrong, and you know it. She's a good girl, and you take her for granted. If you think something's going on between us, you're crazy. She stays in this house every single day, afraid to even go outside. What kind of life is that? Who put that fear in her, Jordan?" He pressed harder, and I saw Jordan wince. But he didn't answer. "Today's Maddie's birthday, and once again, you failed her. She's here all alone in a place no one should raise their kid, and you don't even care. You probably didn't even know today was her birthday. So once again, I'm making sure she's taken care of—not because it's my job, but because you're not doing yours."

Ashton got up, and Jordan jumped to his feet. He kept his distance, but stayed on guard.

"Don't tell me what I should and shouldn't be doing. This is my business, not yours. Why don't you figure out your own life instead of trying to stick your nose in everyone else's? Oh, that's right—you don't have a life. You have to depend on cousin Cody to bail you out because you have nothing."

Jordan turned to me, sneering as I cowered, holding Hope against me. "Did your Prince Charming tell you he just got out of the slammer? Seems he's quite the Robin Hood, stealing from the rich to give to the poor. Except he's really just supporting his nasty coke habit, and giving all his money to the poor dealers." He turned back to Ashton. "So, is Cody hooking you up with the good stuff now that you're out? Are you here so you can sponge off your rich cousin?"

"You don't know anything about me, dude, so don't even start."

"And you don't know anything about me, fucker."

"Maybe not, but I do know Cody wants you out, and I'll be glad to escort you off the property."

"You're lying. Cody has me heading up teams next harvest. He's putting me in charge. It's you who won't have a job."

"Wait," I said, daring to speak up. "I thought we were getting out of here?"

"Not now, Maddie," Jordan warned.

"If we're staying, then what have you been doing all this time?" I prodded.

"Shut your mouth!" Jordan started toward me, but Ashton was on him again. This time Jordan put his hands up, signaling he wouldn't hit back. Ashton let go, but stayed close.

"If I ever hear of you mistreating her again, I'll take care of you myself. Do you understand?" Ashton turned to me. "I'm leaving, but I'm only a few yards away in the warehouse. If he does anything, you come get me. Got it?"

I couldn't look at him. I could only imagine what Jordan was thinking. I kept my eyes on the ground until I heard the front door slam and Ashton's footsteps on the ramp. I counted to one hundred, willing the tears back as I held my breath. Hope's face was pressed against my chest as she breathed heavy. Her little eyes were open as she sucked on her fingers. *This is no life for her.*

"Come on, baby, let's get ready for bed," I murmured. She nodded. I felt sick. *How could I let us get here?* I hated that she'd seen any of this. I allowed this to continue.

I put her on the bed, then turned to get her towel from the bathroom. I was met by Jordan's fist. I didn't even have a chance to cry out before he had me by the hair and threw me on the ground.

"Daddy, no!" Hope cried.

"Jordan, please," I pleaded as he stood over me. He answered by kicking me in the stomach. I felt it everywhere: my toes, my scalp, my fingers. The kick radiated through me, knocking the wind out of me. As I saw him pull his foot back again, I curled into a ball, turning away from him while protecting my head with my hands. His foot met my shoulders and back over and over as I screamed for him to stop.

"I always knew you were fucking around on me," he hissed, followed by another kick. He left me there, and I thought maybe it was over. I scrambled to my feet and went to go for Hope, but he grabbed me again. I heard Hope screaming as he pulled me into the bedroom where he could teach me a lesson without her watching. I fought him, trying to keep him from dragging me in there. It was always worse in there. Once in the bedroom, there were no rules. I grabbed at his shirt, trying to make myself heavy. His shirt ripped in my hands as I pulled on it.

"Let go of me, you fucking bitch," he growled, slamming me into the wall. I went limp, my head throbbing as I saw stars. He pulled me the rest of the way into the room and threw me on the bed. I immediately went into a fetal position, my heart pounding as he slammed and locked the door. Hope didn't even know how to open doors, yet he made sure no one could reach us.

I stared at the wall as he called me a dirty whore, accusing me of cheating on him and telling me I was nothing without him. As he screamed at me, I heard him unbuckling his belt, then whipping it across the bed. He didn't hit me, but I flinched as it snapped next to my head.

"I should really teach you a lesson with this," he said, whipping the belt on the bed again. I flinched, then rolled over so I wasn't facing him. I didn't want to see him, and didn't want him to see me. If he was going to beat me, I wanted him to just do it and get it over with so that maybe he'd leave and I could recover without him. Hope was crying in the front room, and my heart ached for her. I couldn't do anything about it. Any move could make him turn on me again. I listened to his every move, trying to be ready for the next time he came at me. I heard him in the closet, and then the clinking of bottles from the stash he kept there. He took a long swig, and then I braced myself as he got on the bed.

"Here," he demanded. I jumped when I felt the cool glass pressed against my skin. I was afraid to look at him, but I did. He pushed the bottle in my direction. I took it and drank, the spicy rum burning my throat and warming my belly. It was both revolting and relieving. I handed it back, and he took another long drink. I shook my head the next time he tried to give it to me. I knew if I drank more, it would stop my hands from shaking, my body from shivering, my stomach from clenching up. It might make my shoulders relax, my body open, my mind forget.

It might help me to forgive him one more time, and I didn't want to. I wanted to remember this one forever. I was tired of forgetting.

He finished off the bottle, placing it on the side of the bed. It toppled over and dropped on the floor without breaking. Then he turned to me.

"Take off your clothes," he slurred, unbuttoning his pants.

"Jordan," I whispered. I could still hear Hope sobbing in the front room. *Hold tight, baby. It's almost over.*

He pulled down my pants for me. I didn't fight, too petrified to do anything. Tears rolled down my cheeks as he forced my legs open and climbed on top of me. I stayed still as he crushed me with his full weight, thrusting inside me. I wasn't Maddie. I wasn't even human, only a receptacle. It was better than his hands. It was better than being thrown at the wall. It was better than being kicked or beaten with a belt. I never said no, so it wasn't even rape. *Right?* He was my boyfriend. We had a baby together. He was no longer beating me. It was just sex. *It's almost over. It's almost over. It's almost over.*

It was over.

He rolled off me, barely lifting his head as he hit the pillow. I didn't move, but dared to look in his direction.

"You happy, you fucking cunt? I just fucked you like the whore you are." He closed his eyes.

I felt the heat rising inside me. It started out small, a tiny pebble gnawing at my insides. But slowly, it grew into a fireball, inflaming the blood coursing through my veins.

The more I looked at his resting face, the angrier I became. My nose throbbed; I was sure he'd broken it. My body ached from being kicked and from clenching my muscles for so long. His words echoed through my brain, words I didn't deserve. I'd done nothing! Today was my birthday, the one day I should have been taken care of. Instead, he beat me up, and then he took my body without my consent.

I was done being his victim.

***

As soon as I heard his first snore, I was up. I moved cautiously, afraid of waking him. I figured he'd stay asleep from the alcohol, but I didn't want to take any chances. I pulled on my pants, then packed a bag with a few extra clothes, mine and Hope's. Once it was full, I crept to the door and slowly turned the lock. I peeked over my shoulder, watching his face for movement. He was out cold.

In the front room, Hope was asleep, her face on her pillow, bottom in the air. I felt terrible knowing she'd cried herself to sleep. *Never again, baby. I promise.* I left her there and tiptoed to the kitchen, searching for food I could take with us. We had a long drive ahead. I paused, my eyes sweeping over the knives on the counter. I reached for the largest one, wondering what it would feel like to plunge it into his chest, if I could do it without him waking. I could be free of him forever. The thought was so tempting, my hand shook with anticipation.

Do it, I heard a voice say inside me. I felt the pull coming from my belly, as if there were some magnetic force drawing me back to finish what he'd started. *Do it, and make him pay for what he's done to you.*

"No," I said into the stillness, setting the knife down. I wanted to follow through. But if I did, then what? If I failed, he'd kill me. If I succeeded, I'd go to jail. Either way, Hope would be without her mother. Either way, he'd win.

I put on my shoes, then found Hope's. Before I woke her, I searched for Jordan's car keys—no, MY car keys. They weren't in his jacket or on any of the counters. I slipped my shoes off and crept back to the room, hearing his snores. I glowered at the way his chest rose and fell, wishing I had the guts and stupidity to do him in. I pulled out the keys from his pants pocket, then searched for money, but came up empty. I had no idea where he hid it, and I knew I was running out of time. I looked at him one last time, burning his face into my memory. No longer would I think of him as anything but a monster. I was done making excuses for him. I was done believing he'd take care of me. I was done waiting for him to fulfill his promises. I was done waiting for him to change.

I was done.

I put my shoes back on, and then did the same for Hope. She stirred.

"Mama?" she whispered.

"Shhh, baby, we have to be really quiet. Daddy's sleeping." I glanced at the clock. It was nearly 1 a.m. I slipped her jacket on and picked her up. Balancing her on one hip, I slung the bag over the opposite shoulder and opened the door. A blast of cold air met me, followed by a few snowflakes. By the next morning, everything would probably be white. I wasn't sad to miss it.

The full moon peeked out from the scattered clouds, lighting the way to the car. I unlocked the doors quietly and put Hope in her car seat and the bag at her feet, then sat in the driver's seat. My whole body was a heartbeat, and my breath came out in tufts as I put the key in the ignition. I knew someone would hear me start the car. Once I turned the key, I had to move. If anyone tried to stop me, I was done for. I took a deep breath in.

"1…" I whispered, peering into the warehouse windows. They were dark.

"2…" A look in the rearview mirror proved Jordan was still asleep. All the lights in the bungalow were off.

"3." I turned the key and immediately shifted into reverse. I didn't dare look at the windows again as I put the car in drive and moved forward. But I slammed the heel of my hand on the steering wheel when I came to the gate. It was shut. I'd have to get out and open it. I put the car into park, then got out and sprinted to the gate. It was chained, padlocked in place.

"Dammit!" I cried, no longer caring if I could be heard. I raced back to the car, turning it off and snatching the keys. I tried every one of them on the lock, but none worked. If Jordan had a key that fit this lock, he didn't keep it on this key chain.

"What are you doing?"

I whipped around and saw Ashton standing there. His eyes widened when he caught sight of my face. He reached out to touch my cheek, and I turned my head away.

"The light is green," I whispered. I could only guess what I looked like, but knew it wasn't pretty. He nodded.

"Let me get that for you." He used his key on the padlock, then turned the hitch and let it swing wide.

"Thank you." I turned to leave.

"Maddie." He came over to me and put his arms around me. I stiffened, my automatic reaction as I worried about what Jordan would think. But I was leaving. It no longer mattered what he thought. I relaxed, leaning my head against Ashton. I felt his lips touch the top of my head, lingering for a moment.

"I'm sorry," he whispered.

"Sorry? What for?"

"I wasn't there to stop him. I should have stayed. I should have known he'd take it out on you."

"How could you have known?"

"I just should have. I never should have left. I should have helped you leave him right then."

"Ashton, don't blame yourself. If anything, I'm to blame. I stayed far too long. I believed in him too long." I stopped, shaking my head. "I was so stupid."

"No, you weren't." He lifted my chin so I was looking at him. "You trusted him, because that's what you're supposed to do when someone promises to take care of you. He failed you. You deserve so much more."

I wasn't sure what I deserved. I was damaged goods. I'd made a mess of everything. I'd vowed to give Hope a good life, and hadn't lived up to that promise.

"I better go," I whispered. "He's passed out, and I don't know how long he'll stay asleep."

Ashton nodded, and let me go. I started to move toward the car again when he took my hand, pulled me to him, and kissed me. I let him. I even kissed him back. But when we broke apart, I knew this first kiss was also our last.

"Goodbye, Maddie," he told me. "I never want to see you again."

I smiled, tears filling my eyes. I wondered how things would have worked out had we met under different circumstances. Ashton was a good guy. He was charming and easy to look at. He'd helped us, and had been nice to talk with. I felt safe when he was around. But we were never meant to be. Allowing anything to happen between us would keep me tied to this place—to this life—and I wanted to leave it all behind.

"Goodbye, Ashton," I said. "I never want to see you again." He grinned, his eyes growing shiny. He stepped back as I got into the car. I glanced in the rearview mirror as I drove away, watching as he stood there, getting smaller by the second. One bend on the road, and he was gone. Ashton, the farm, Cody, Jordan… all gone.

I breathed easier once I reached the freeway. I knew I had hours in front of me, but it was one step closer to being home.

"Home," I whispered. I still hadn't decided what that meant. More than anything, I wanted to run back to Charlie's house. Did I dare? I'd been so terrible to him. What if I'd crossed the line for the last time? What if I got there and he never wanted to see me again?

It was more than that, though. I didn't believe I deserved his forgiveness. He'd been right all this time, and I'd been ridiculously wrong.

I stopped for the bathroom two hours into the drive, keeping my hood on and my eyes low as the guy handed me the key at the gas station. After we were done, I looked in the mirror for the first time and immediately regretted it. There was blood in my hair, and my eye was swollen. My nose appeared crooked, and I wondered if it would ever be straight again. I looked ugly, ruined.

When I returned the key, I hurried to my car. I looked at the gas gauge, and knew I wouldn't be able to go much further. It was ironic to be at a gas station, yet unable to get the gas I needed. I only had a quarter-tank left, and so much more road to go.

But stopping was suicide.

My gas light came on as the sky began to lighten. I ran out of gas when the sun crested the hills. I was lucky it happened near a turnout. The morning commute had already started, and cars sailed past me without a care. I stayed there for a moment. I thought about who I could call, knowing I only had two options—Charlie or Jace. I could almost hear Jordan's voice in my head, calling me a whore for even thinking about calling Jace. Maybe he was right. I'd left Jace, and then fell back in with Jordan. Plus, I'd kissed Ashton at the farm. Now, I was considering calling Jace again, asking him to bail me out when I'd left without a word.

None of this mattered; Jace probably thought I hated him. I had no right to call him. But I couldn't bring myself to call Charlie.

The engine whined as I turned the key, but refused to turn over. I pulled the keys out and threw them across the dash in frustration. The noise was louder than I anticipated and I glanced in the back seat. Hope was still sleeping.

With my phone in hand, I got out of the car and walked over to the passenger side so I wasn't next to the busy highway. The ocean spread out in front of me, a stark blue under the lightening morning sky. I looked down at the phone in my hands. My sleeves hiked up my arms, and I pulled them down to cover the bruises out of habit.

I didn't know if he'd answer. He had no reason to answer. I was afraid he'd ignore my call. Worse, I was afraid he'd answer and give me hell for the way I disappeared. But I had no choice.

His name wasn't on my phone. I wasn't that dumb. But I knew his number by heart. I touched each digit, pausing before I hit the final one. Then I held the phone to my ear and waited.

"Hello?"

Today

Ruined

A knock jolts me awake. Hope is still awake, hypnotized by some show on television. It's been so long since we've watched TV. I'm glad to see it's a kids show, and that it didn't switch to something inappropriate while I was napping.

The knock sounds again, and my hands shake. The clock says it's 5:15 p.m., hours after Jace was supposed to be here. It's probably him, but part of me worries it's

Jordan, or someone looking for me on Jordan's behalf, or anyone who will rob me of the safety I'm so close to once Jace rescues me. But will I really be rescued? I know the past will still haunt me after the bruises fade.

"Maddie." His voice is low behind the door, and I jump up and open it. *Jace.* He looks the same and different at the same time. His smile evaporates, replaced by rage when he sees my face.

"What did he do to you?" Jace demands. I look away and step back so he can come into the room, catching a whiff of the pizza he's carrying. My stomach aches in anticipation. I want to pounce on the food, but know he wants an answer.

"Let's just say it's been a long six months, and I made a big mistake." His expression remains dark, and I can see the anger in his eyes. "Jace, it's okay."

"Like hell it is," he says. "Why didn't you call me sooner? I could have helped you!" I nod toward Hope. *We'll talk about this later,* I say with my eyes. His expression softens and he gives a slight nod. He sets the pizza down on the table, then turns around with a fake smile.

"Hope!"

She finally notices his presence and crawls into my lap, hiding her face.

"Looks like she's forgotten me," Jace says. He shrugs as if this were normal, but I can tell he's disappointed. Hope lifts her head.

"KK here?" she whispers. I shoot Jace a grin.

"She remembers you." I turn back to Hope. "She's not here now, but I bet we see her soon, maybe even tomorrow."

"Definitely tomorrow," Jace agrees.

We eat the pizza, and it's like food for the soul. I notice that Jace only takes two pieces while I polish off four. I could eat more, but force myself to stop once I feel human again.

"Happy belated birthday, by the way," Jace says, making a face. "But I guess it hasn't been that happy."

"It is now." I touch his hand, but pull away when my skin touches his. I feel like Jordan is on my shoulder. As comfortable as I feel around Jace, I also feel wrong to have called him. I don't need a knight in shining armor. That's all I ever do, look for someone to save me. Except, I couldn't have gone any further without his help. Jordan would have found me and made me pay for leaving with Hope.

I wish I knew how to be more independent instead of making huge messes of my life.

"We need to talk about what happened," Jace says, interrupting my thoughts. I know we do, and using Hope as a buffer is lame. She was there, she saw everything. Talking about it in front of her won't damage her any more than what she witnessed. Now that I've eaten, I realize I actually *want* to tell him. I *need* to get all this out. I've been through hell, and surrounded by people who didn't care, and who thought this was normal. But this wasn't normal, and I didn't belong there.

And so I spill. His face falls as I describe how everything went downhill in such a short amount of time…too long of a time. I feel ashamed that I stayed, that I couldn't predict how bad it would get when it was so obvious. Looking at Jace's reaction, I want to hide and pretend none of this happened. But it also feels relieving to get all this out.

"He told me if I ever left him, he'd not only hunt me down, he'd kill whoever tried to help me," I say. "He tracked me on my phone until I threw it into the ocean. He knows I'm gone, that I'm in California. I saw his phone's location, and he was following me. He doesn't know where I am, or he would have found me by now, but I'm sure he knows where I'm going. It's only a matter of time before he finds me, and when he does, I'm afraid I've put you in danger, or Charlie. Oh God. Charlie!" I realize Jordan has probably already reached Charlie by now.

"You know we need to file a police report, right?" Jace says, and I cower. I feel like that will make things worse. I know it's ridiculous, and I *should* call the police, but I'm more afraid of how Jordan will react if I do.

"I can't." Jace starts to protest, but I stop him. "Please don't fight me on this. I know I should, but I'm afraid."

Jace embraces me, and I close my eyes and inhale. It's the same scent as always—citrus and soap. It calms me.

"If you're worried about Charlie's safety, something needs to be done."

"I'll call Fátima."

"What can she do that the cops can't?" he asks.

"She has brothers, four of them. They're big guys, and they don't always worry about what's right or wrong. They'll keep Charlie safe until... Well, they'll keep him safe."

I stare at my phone. Calling Jace was one thing. I don't know what Fátima will say once I get on the line. I hand Jace the phone.

"I can't."

"What do you mean?"

"Please don't make me explain. I just can't. Do it for me? Please? Just tell her you've heard something that makes you think Charlie is in trouble. Tell her he needs protection."

Sadness fills his eyes. I can't handle it, and I turn away.

"Oh, Maddie," he whispers. "I hope Jordan finds me. Then I can repay him for every damn thing he did to you."

"I hope he never finds you," I say. "The scariest part wasn't that he hit, but that he was unpredictable. I never knew which Jordan I was getting when he came home. If he comes across you, or Charlie, or anyone else I love, I don't know what he'll do to any of you."

"I hope he finds me," Jace repeats firmly, looking me in the eye. "Now, what's Fátima's number?"

Once he's on the phone with Fátima, he relays everything I told him to say. I can tell she's asking for more information, but he avoids answering her questions. When he hangs up, I look at him expectantly.

"She says she's sending her brothers over, like you said she would. Charlie's safe for now. But don't think for a second I'm letting up on this. The police need to get involved."

"I know," I say. "But not yet."

"Fine, but we need to take photos of your injuries," he says.

"What? Are you kidding?"

"We need evidence of what he did, and we need to do it now while it's fresh. I'm sorry."

I know he's right. Still, I want to curl up into nothing. He's never seen me naked. Now he's about to see my body for the first time, covered in bruises.

"Maddie, it's just for the police report, when we file one. You need as much evidence as possible, especially since you'll want a restraining order."

"And I'm sure he'll follow that," I mutter.

"Hey." He puts his hand on my knee to get my attention. "It's something. I know it's not perfect, and not a sure way to keep him away. But it's one more barrier that can help you, okay?"

"Okay," I whisper.

"You'll let me take the pictures?" I nod, unable to say the word *yes*.

We go into the bathroom, keeping the door open so we can see Hope, but making sure she can't see our photo session. He turns his back as I undress.

"I'm keeping my bra and underwear on."

"That's fine. Are you ready?"

"Almost."

I look in the mirror. I want to see what he'll see first. I'm shocked and intrigued by the bruises. So many bruises. Dark purple marks cover my back. There's a large one near my shoulder, and one near my hip. The rest are smaller, but still dark. One large bruise fades from my side to my belly, where Jordan kicked me in the stomach. I lean closer to the mirror. My right eye is swollen almost completely shut, surrounded by a deep bruise. My eyeball is completely red, as if a blood vessel burst. It must be so hard for Jace to look at me. I touch my nose, wincing as I try to press against it. I'll have to see a doctor about this one, I know. I touch the gash on my head. There's dried blood in my hair since I haven't yet taken a shower.

"Maddie."

I turn. I can see Jace is trying to be strong, but I can't miss the wobble in his lip.

"I'll be quick, okay?"

I nod, and he starts snapping pictures with his cellphone. He gets my face first, taking a photo of each bruise. He moves to my body next, taking one picture as a whole, then focusing on the rest of my injuries, one at a time. His hands are shaking when he finishes, and I take them into mine.

"It's okay," I say, and he gives a short laugh.

"I'm the one who's supposed to be comforting you." He smiles, but his lip is still trembling. "Oh, Maddie."

I hold him as he starts to shake. He sets his phone on the counter, and puts his arms around my waist, laying the top of his head on my chest as he collects himself. Then he lifts his head and looks into my eyes. He leans in, touching his lips to my nose, my eye, and finally the wound on my head. He kisses each bruise on my body, touching me lightly as if his lips could hurt what Jordan already injured. I want to let him continue, but keep feeling like Jordan is watching. I want it to feel right, but it feels all wrong.

"I can't," I say, stepping back. My eyes fill with tears because I'm *so angry* that I can't accept Jace's compassion and tenderness. I'm *so angry* that I can't accept this kind of love because I'm completely broken. I'm *so angry* because I had a chance to start something with Jace all those months ago, and I threw it away for the man who ruined me—and now I'm not sure I can ever be mended.

"It's okay," Jace tells me. "I shouldn't have been so forward. You need time to heal. I just assumed...I was being too forward."

"It's not that," I protest, but he holds his hand up.

"You've been through a lot. I want to be here for you. You don't need to explain anything. Just let me help you."

"Okay," I whisper.

"I'm going into the other room to hang with Hope for a while. You're going to take a bath and relax. Don't worry about anything; I have everything under control."

He squeezes my hand, giving me a small smile before leaving. I'm left alone with my reflection in the mirror, and a sinking feeling in my heart. *Will it always be this way?*

Will I always feel like everything I'm doing is wrong and I could get in trouble?

I run the hot water, using the motel shampoo to make a bubble bath. When I step in, I realize how tired my body is. Everything aches. I sink into the water and close my eyes, scooting down so my head is submerged. All I can hear is my heartbeat. I open my eyes and stare at the ceiling, breathing into the silence. I pretend I'm the only one left on earth. There's no Jordan, no Cody, and no Ashton. There's no Charlie, no Fátima, and no Jace. My parents don't exist, and neither do any of my classmates. Not even Hope is there. It's just me, with no one around that can hurt me, and no one that I can ruin with my brokenness.

When the water cools, I wrap myself in a towel. I pause at the mirror and look at my face once more. I wish I'd brought makeup to cover the damage, the way Bethany taught me. I now see how sick that was. It had been so normalized, as if this was what was done after someone you love beats the snot out of you. I realize it was normal for *her*. It had started to become normal for me. I *don't want* it to be normal. But I still wish for makeup so I can spare Jace from seeing me this way.

My clothes are in the other room, and I have no choice but to go out there half-naked to get them. I smile at Hope curled up in the bed, Jace leaning next to her. She can barely keep her eyes open, but is trying as the TV continues to flash in front of her.

"I've been trying to keep her awake so she can go potty before bed," Jace says. I'm warmed by how much he knows about raising little girls, but it also makes me sad. I'd refused a relationship with Jace because I'd decided he wasn't ready to take on the responsibility of a toddler. I figured he was too young, that it wasn't fair to him. But with Jordan, I didn't hesitate. Jordan was Hope's daddy, so all this stuff was supposed to come naturally. It didn't. If he were here now, he wouldn't have thought about Hope needing to potty before bed. He didn't think about anyone but himself.

"Thank you," I tell him. "I'll take her in now." I coax her into the bathroom, and she sleepily complies. I follow her with the bag of our belongings. As she potties, I put on some sweats. Then I help her into her pajamas and brush her teeth. I study her face as I do, realizing how old she is now. She's only three, but she's been through more than most adults. I feel guilty over everything she witnessed, and try to find comfort that I'm trying to make things right by going home. But even this feels wrong. Everything feels wrong. *I'm a horrible mom. I messed up.*

She doesn't even argue about getting into bed. The TV is off and Jace is fiddling with his phone while I tuck her in and give her a kiss.

"Goodnight, princess," I whisper as she closes her eyes. My body feels sedated from the bath, and I'm equal parts relaxed, sore, and wanting to forget everything about Oregon. I get into bed and turn on my pillow toward Jace on the other bed. He puts his phone down and leans across the space separating our beds to give me a kiss on the cheek. After he turns the light out, I hear him go into the bathroom to get ready for bed. I'm drifting in and out of sleep when he comes back, the squeak of his bedsprings filling the silence of the room. I'm unable to stay awake, yet I can't fall asleep. Everything about last night comes back to me in flashes. The way Jordan punched me. The way he took me down in front of Hope. How he slammed me into the wall. How he raped me.

I realize now that's what he did. He *raped* me. I never said the word *no*. But I never consented. It woke me up. I would have left him eventually. Maybe. I think I would have left him. Maybe I still would have stayed, believing he had another way to get us out. But when he raped me, I knew I couldn't stay. It wasn't a good place for me, and it wasn't a good place for our daughter. His harsh words, his abuse, his lies proved he didn't love me—he never had and never would. Nothing was going to change; why had I thought it would?

"Are you okay?" Jace whispers. I realize I'm crying. I sniff, wiping my face with the blanket.

"Not really," I whisper back, which only makes me cry harder.

"Come here," he says. I hesitate, afraid of what this could lead to. But I know I need him to hold me. My violated body needs to feel nurtured, cared for. I need Jace to undo the torment Jordan has left me with. I get out of bed and crawl into Jace's arms.

"I need this to not mean anything," I whisper. "I need you to hold me, but not because you want me, or love me, or need me."

"Tonight I'm your friend. And tomorrow, and every day after that. I'm not here for any other reason."

I cry even more at this. Jace holds me, tightening his arms around me as I shudder in his embrace. He doesn't do anything more than that. He doesn't tell me everything will be okay, or kiss away my pain, or try to get me to talk. He just holds me and lets me cry.

I'm right where I need to be. I can finally let go.

Home

It takes me a moment to realize where I am when I wake up. The first thing I notice is that I'm warm. This is different from the drafty chill I usually wake to. The bed feels different. It's not lumpy, the sheets are smooth, and the blankets on top of me are heavier. They smell different. They're not musty. I inhale the scent of the fabric, noting the fragrance of detergent and…is that coffee? I'm in that place between sleep and awake, when I know I'm through sleeping but my eyes refuse to open. It feels good to be asleep. But that coffee…

I force my eyes open, blinking at the small amount of light coming in through the curtains. I realize where I am. The motel. California. Jace.

I sit up with a start. My head spins, and I wince.

"Here." Jace stands up and places a cup of coffee in my hands, waiting until I have a firm grip on it before sitting back on the bed. I take a sip. Never has coffee tasted so good. My whole body feels heavy. Every movement hurts. In the dim light, I notice Hope's still asleep.

"What time is it?" I ask, looking at the clock at the same time. It's just past seven—still early, but at least the sun is up. .

"They have breakfast in the lobby," Jace says. "I brought back some food so we can eat before getting on the road. I'm sure you want to get back."

Do I? I was anxious to get away. Now where am I going? I want to see Charlie, but I'm afraid. But if I don't go there, where do I go?

Jace and I pick through the pastries he brought, and I choose one with lemon curd in the middle, and a yogurt to go with it. The sugary treats are hardly the breakfast of champions, but you can't beat free. Well, sort of free.

"I'll pay you back for the room as soon as I have a job," I say, wondering how I'd find a place to live, get someone to watch Hope, and find a job at the same time.

"You think I'll let you give me money?"

"I'm not your problem."

"No, you're my friend." He gives me a pointed look. "My only payment is knowing you're safe, and getting to see you every day."

"*Every* day?"

"Sometimes even twice a day," he says. I roll my eyes, but I know he's telling the truth.

Once Hope is awake, she powers through a pastry while I put our belongings into the bag. It takes all of five minutes. Same for Hope, who is reaching for another pastry. I try to coax her into eating a hard-boiled egg instead, but when she insists on the sugary treat, I cave and give her half.

"You know she'll be a pill in about an hour, right?" I say.

Jace shrugs. "We'll just get her more sugar."

"Jace!"

We leave the motel room and put our stuff in Jace's car. I look over my shoulder the whole time, wondering if Jordan is waiting to ambush us. I don't breathe easy until we're on the freeway. With Jace behind the wheel, Hope in her car seat, and me sitting in the passenger seat, everything feels somewhat normal. I feel better than I've felt in a long time. I don't have to worry about protecting myself. I don't have to watch everything I do. I can relax and let Jace take over. I don't have to be *on*.

I must have slept half the drive. I feel guilty when I wake up, seeing that Petaluma is only two hours away. I try to apologize, but Jace won't have it.

"You obviously need your rest," he says. We stop for a bathroom break, and then a real breakfast of eggs and sausage. Hope is warmed up to Jace and is talking up a storm.

"Where's Daddy?" Hope asks, and I feel my chest tighten as I realize I'll have to work out answers about her father and all we've been through. Everything feels so messy. None of this is normal. I look at Jace, but he can't answer this one for me. He knows it, judging by the way he averts his eyes. I'm sure he'd rather me rip the Band-Aid off immediately by telling her the truth—she'll never see her daddy again. At least, I hope that's the truth. Everything is so uncertain. I don't even know where we're going to live.

"Uh…" I search for the right words, not wanting to explain too much, and not wanting to lie. "Uh, he's probably, uh…" *Why is this so hard?*

"He's not here," Jace answers, and I look at him gratefully. This appears to satisfy her. Still, I'll need to work out what to tell her the next time. He's working? He's at home? He's hopefully driven off a cliff and plunged into the ocean?

I feel dumb. I can't even think up a single answer for my daughter's questions about her dad.

"Come on, guys, two more hours and we're home," Jace says cheerfully as we gather our things from the table.

"Where's home?" I whisper to him. He squeezes my hand.

"My house, for now," he says. I'm grateful I don't need to explain myself. He understands.

***

It's mid-afternoon when I see the familiar sights of Petaluma. It looks like home. I inhale, and the ripe scent of manure fills my nose, welcoming me back to this cozy farm town. Even the smell is home to me.

Hope is sleeping when we pull into Jace's driveway. It's a two-story house with a lawn and a tree with a swing. Flowers line the walkway. The mailbox is quaint, shaped like a miniature barn. I'd only been here once, and it seems like a lifetime ago.

Jace carries our stuff in while I unbuckle Hope. She remains mostly asleep as I pick her up, but starts to wake up as I walk her to the house. Once inside, there's no keeping her asleep. A small dog greets us, barking as it jumps on my legs.

"Popcorn, down!" Jace demands, nudging the little white dog with his shin. I laugh.

"You got a dog and named it Popcorn? That's its name?"

"We let Kayci name him. With the way he jumps on everyone, well, it fits."

Hope is fully awake, straining to see the dog.

"Is he good with kids?" I ask as Hope tries to get down. The question is answered when Kayci runs into the room and throws herself at Popcorn. The dog rolls over and takes her enthusiastic greeting, licking the top of her head as Kayci lies on him.

"Jace!" she cries, and leaves the dog to run at him. He drops the bags on the ground and catches her.

"How's my baby sis?" he asks, and she squeals as he tosses her up in the air. Hope seems to have lost her shyness completely, because she's soon at Jace's knees, begging to have a turn.

"Maddie," I hear a woman say, and I turn as Jace's mom comes in the room. She's smiling as she gives me a hug, and I feel self-conscious, knowing what my face looks like. But she acts as if the bruises aren't there. Jace probably texted her a warning. "It's so good to finally meet you. I'm Grace. Have you guys eaten?"

"We stopped for breakfast a few hours ago, but we're hungry again," Jace says as he pries himself from the girls.

After Grace helps me unpack, we all end up in the kitchen, enjoying what Tom, Jace's stepdad, calls "hot dog sandwiches"—grilled cheese with sliced hot dogs in between—plus bowls of chicken and vegetable soup. The food warms me from the inside out, and I'm embarrassed when the tears start to fall again. I wonder if everything will make me emotional.

"It's okay," Grace says. "You're safe now." Of course, this only makes me cry harder. I feel everything I've kept bottled coming at me at once. As I let down my guard, the shock of what I've been through washes over me. Now that I'm safe, now that I no longer need to be on guard or protect myself, I can finally breathe again. I can finally be at ease. I can let others take care of me.

And so, I sleep for weeks.

Sleep isn't quite the right word. It's more like I become part of the couch for the first few weeks I'm back. The world moves around me, and I remain still. My body shuts down and I can't bring myself to get up. I feel like I'm disappearing from everyone's view. I hear Jace's worried whispers when he thinks I'm not listening, and Grace's reassurance, "She just needs time to recover." She and Tom parent Hope. I barely eat, even though Jace tries to coax me. I can't even muster a smile for Hope: she eventually moves around me as if I'm not there. I don't care. I hate to admit it, but I don't have it in me. If I suddenly stopped breathing, it would feel like a blessing. I drift in and out of sleep all day, staring at the wall when I'm awake. At night, my experiences haunt me. I feel Jordan's hands around my neck, I'm violated by Cody, or lost in a field of overgrown marijuana plants. I freeze to death in a dirty bungalow. I even see Hope grow up in my visions, looking something like Bethany—beautiful, but with eyes that tell a different story.

The one thing that keeps me from withdrawing completely is my fear that Jordan will find us. I know he tried to follow us, but there's been no word on where he is. Sometimes I'm terrified. Other times I hope he'll find me and finish me forever. But I also know if he finds me, he'll find everyone I love and make them pay for what I've done to him. If he finds me, I won't be the only one going down.

"No one's seen him around Charlie's house," Jace reports. He never says Jordan's name, as if hearing it will push me deeper into depression. We're in the new year now. The Christmas decorations are gone and the sky outside is as gray as I feel. This was the first year I missed Christmas. I bought nothing for Hope, or anyone else. Hope never knew. Jace's family made sure she was properly spoiled while I just disappeared a little bit more.

Jace lets me know how Charlie's doing, though he's sworn that Charlie has no idea I'm here. Fátima's brothers are no longer securing the property daily, but Jace says they check in every few days to make sure things are all right. I'm fuzzy on how Jace gets his information, and don't have the energy to understand better. According to him, Fátima shares everything she knows with Charlie. I'm sure there's more to the story, since Fátima doesn't know I'm back, either. But trying to understand is like trying to get up off the couch. I just can't.

"I wish you'd let me call Charlie and tell him you're back," Jace says.

"You promised you wouldn't." I turn to face the wall so he can't look at my face. I can't see Charlie, especially now. He gave me the world, and I traded it in for a life of poverty, lawlessness, and abuse. He would hate that I introduced Hope to a world like this. I'd failed her. I'd also failed Charlie. I couldn't face him.

"I'm not calling him," Jace reassures me. "I'm just saying I wish you'd let me. I know he'd want to take care of you."

I roll back over and glare at him.

"If you're tired of me being here, just tell me." He places his hand on my arm, but I angrily shake him off.

"You know that's not true. I want you to be happy, and I'm glad you're here. But Charlie loves you. He'd want to help you. Let me call him."

I shake my head, then close my eyes to fight the tears. It doesn't work. They squeeze out and soak my pillow. Jace touches my arm again, and this time I let him.

"I messed up," I whisper. Jace says nothing, just continues to rub my arm. "He did everything to help me, and I stabbed him in the back. Even if he could forgive me, I don't deserve it. He was the best person in my life, and I let him down."

"But Maddie, don't you—"

"No."

"Maddie, I—"

"No!" I shout, sitting up. My head aches from the sudden movement. I lean back and close my eyes. "Stop trying to get me to call him. I'm not, and that's final."

"So, you'll never see him again?" Never seems like such a strong word. Regretfully, I nod my head. "So, if Charlie got really sick and was dying, you wouldn't go see him?" My eyes fly open.

"What are you saying, Jace?"

"I'm not saying anything."

"Is Charlie sick?"

"Well, he's not a young man," Jace says. "He's been through a lot this year, with Viola passing away, and you leaving. It's only natural it would be hard on him. Any day could be his last."

"Why didn't you tell me?" I jump to my feet. "We need to go now."

"Go where?" Jace asks.

"To Charlie's, you idiot! I need to see him!" I run to the corner of the room and pull a sweatshirt on, then start putting on my shoes. It suddenly isn't important I've let him down. I need to make this right. I can't have him die thinking that I hate him. I love him! He's more of a father to me than my own. I have to let him know.

"Maddie," Jace says. He's smiling, and I can feel my insides tie up in anger.

"You think this is funny?" I pick up a shoe and throw it at him. He ducks and it hits the wall.

"Calm down." Even his eyes are laughing.

"I'm not calm! And I wouldn't even be talking to you now if I didn't have to rely on you for a ride. So shut up and just take me there."

"Maddie."

The deep voice resonates through me, and tears spring to my eyes. I look in the entryway and see Charlie. For a moment, I can't say anything. Every wrong thing I've done to this man wraps around me, and I can hardly breathe. But seeing him, I'm home. I want to run to him and let him undo everything I've messed up. I want to beg him to forgive me and spend a lifetime making it up to him. I want to tell him I was wrong, that he's the father I never had, and I owe him everything. But I don't.

Instead, I dissolve into tears, and he comes to me, pulling me into a tight embrace. I shake in his arms, unworthy of his affection. I failed him. I failed everyone. I don't deserve this.

"I'm so sorry," I whisper into his jacket, and he soothes me with shushing sounds.

"Come home," he tells me, his voice firm.

"I can't."

"Why not? I want you there. I want Hope there. I want you to stay for as long as you want. There's still a business you need to help me run, and college courses you need to take. I'll put you in counseling. If you'd like, I'll even set you up in your own apartment. But I want you back in my life, and I want to be able to keep you safe. Please come home."

"Why are you doing this?" I ask. "You tried to tell me he was no good, and I didn't believe you. You were right the whole time. If I'd listened to you, I would have been fine. But I didn't."

"It's all going to be okay," Charlie says.

"How can you say that?" I ask. "I took his daughter. He said he'd kill me and everyone I love if I did that to him. He's just waiting for the perfect moment to do what he promised. I should have filed a police report. I should have had them throw him in jail. Now, we're all in danger."

"We're not, though," Charlie says.

"But—"

"Jace and I filed our own report." I start to protest, but he keeps talking. "With your pictures and what you shared with Jace, we were able to give the police information. But without your statement, they couldn't arrest him. We knew you weren't strong enough, so we talked them into waiting on that. In the meantime, I have a private investigator following him, making sure he never sets foot on my property. Last night, he did."

I gasp, clutching his arm at what he's saying.

"It's okay. The investigator let me know Jordan was headed our way. Jorge got to him before Jordan could make it to the house. He held him there until the police came. He didn't have any weapons on him, so his intent was murky. But they're holding him for twenty-four hours on trespassing charges. This is where you come in."

"I can't see him," I say, looking away.

"I'm not asking you to," Charlie reassures me. "Not yet, at least. But the police need your statement. It could make the case stronger, showing he's been trying to find you and hurt you." He squeezes my hand. "I know this is asking a lot. I know you're not ready. But honey, this is your chance to be free of him for good. You deserve to be safe."

"I don't deserve anything," I mutter.

"Maddie Russo," Charlie barks. I can't look at him, keeping my eyes trained on the ground as he continues. "You are worthy of love. You deserve to be cherished. You deserve a life free from danger, abuse, and mistreatment. You are a wonderful girl and a beautiful person. I will not have some bastard having you believe any different."

"How can you say any of that?" I ask. "I was so terrible to you! Now you have to go to all this trouble so this asshole I brought into our lives doesn't murder us."

"Don't you get it, honey? I love you. I'll always love you. There's nothing you can do that would make me stop loving you. You're my daughter."

His words silence me. I peer at him, waiting for him to realize what he's said. Everything in his expression tells me he meant it. He smiles, taking my hand.

"Thank you...Dad." I try out the word, liking the way it tastes, liking the way it makes me feel. It's been so long since I called anyone that name. My first father stripped away my security, and any warmth left in the word. Charlie gave it back. *Dad*. It fit.

I notice the tears in his eyes, and he chuckles and looks away, wiping his eyes on his sleeve. "I guess you can say the prodigal daughter has returned," he says.

I take the time to shower, since I'm suddenly aware of how long it's been. Knowing I have all this support surrounding me, I feel more confident and determined. I even smile as the water runs over me, thinking how I'll make sure Jordan pays for everything he put me through. When I'm done with him, he'll never be able to hurt anyone again.

We go to the police station, and I give the officer my statement. Even though Jordan's behind bars, I feel uneasy knowing he's near, and sick as I look through the pictures in the file, shocked at how I looked just a month ago. It's embarrassing to know Charlie already saw these photos. I hate that he's seen me looking this way.

When we're done, Jace goes home so Charlie and I can get reacquainted. Over lunch, I tell him everything, all the dark details. It's a relief to talk. I tell him the car has been stripped of its paint, sitting on the side of a highway hundreds of miles away.

"No, it's not," he says. "It's parked in the garage at home, restored, repainted and ready for whenever you want to drive it." He insists I need to go to counseling, and I agree. I'm not surprised that he has a name of a therapist who can see Hope and me first thing Monday morning.

He's aged since I last saw him. His eyes look tired and his skin is pale. He tells me he'd tried to track me, but didn't know where to look. "It never occurred to me he'd take you to a pot farm," Charlie says angrily. "He hurt you, and he exposed your daughter to unimaginable things. I won't stop until he is out of our lives forever."

His statement sounds threatening. *Would he kill Jordan, if it came to it?* Looking at his expression, I'm sure he would. I'm glad we're letting the police handle this.

14

Ash

I move back into Charlie's house. It's bittersweet leaving Jace and his family. I'd spent my whole time with them in a state of depression, and they'd made sure I had the space I needed to heal. Guilt and shame wrap around me once again: I put them through so much on my behalf. Grace waves away my apologies, telling me her home is always open to me.

It's good to be home. I forgot how it felt to have my own bedroom and bath. The first night back, I take an hour-long bath, keeping it hot by continuously adding water. I sleep late the next morning, enjoying the weight of heavy comforters. When I finally get up, Fátima is in the kitchen, pouring herself a cup of coffee. She turns when she hears me.

"Mija!" She crosses the room to envelop me in a hug.

"It's so good to see you," I say. She takes a step back and looks me over.

"You look skinny. You need to eat."

I look at the table filled with pastries, sausage, bagels, and fruit.

"I don't think that will be a problem," I said. "Let me wake Hope first."

Hope's already out of her crib, playing with toys on the ground. It's only a matter of time before she figures out how to use the doorknob.

"I guess it's finally time to get you that big girl bed, huh?" It's been so long since she's been in a crib, anyway.

That morning, we eat until we can't eat anymore. I meet Fátima's brothers officially—Jorge, Jose, Arturo, and Eduardo. They're extremely good looking—and massive. Charlie was in good hands.

I spend the day rediscovering everything I loved about home. Hope and I walk through the skeletal vineyards while I tell her how the vines will transform over the next few months, starting with bud break in the spring. We visit Viola's neglected garden, and I make a mental note of the work I need to do to get it ready for spring. We come inside at lunch for soup and grilled cheese sandwiches. Thanks to Tom, Hope now insists on hot dog sandwiches instead of normal grilled cheese. Then Hope takes a nap while I sit on the couch and look at the walls around me—so glad to be here, the first place I felt unconditional love. I want to shake myself for taking so long to get here.

"Do you have a moment?"

Charlie's standing in the hallway, holding the urn.

"I waited until you came home," he says softly. I get up without speaking and follow him out into the backyard, through the naked vines to the top of the hill. He sits in a space where the vines break, offering a view of the hills on the other side of the valley. I sit next to him, and we look over the valley beyond the property. The breeze is chilly, and I pull my jacket closer around me.

"I'm sorry," I whisper. "I failed you."

"No, sweetheart."

I shake my head, my tears creating hot trails down my cheeks.

"I did," I insist. "Viola died, and I left you. I messed up. You've been so good to me, better than anyone in my whole life, and I let you down." I choke on a sob, hugging my knees to my chest. "I'm so sorry."

Charlie sets the urn down and puts his arm around my shoulders. I try to shake him off, but he grasps me firmly.

I collapse into him, submitting to his embrace as he holds me tightly.

"You didn't know," he says. I try to argue, but he cuts me off. "Yes, you said hurtful things. You were angry; I knew that. You thought you were making the best decision. We all have choices to make in life. Sometimes we choose wisely, and sometimes we choose the path that will teach us a lesson. You've learned a lot while you were gone, more than I'd ever want you to learn. You went through some horrible things. And you survived. Right now, you're still healing. But one day, this hard lesson will lead you to a beautiful new beginning."

I continue to cry against him as he strokes my hair. I try to stop, but I keep going back to the night I left.

"Maddie."

I wipe my eyes and look at him. My whole body aches. I want to disappear. His forgiveness isn't enough. I can't forgive myself.

"I wish you knew what I see when I look at you," he says.

"A mess."

"No, I see a wonderful girl who's been told all her life she's not wanted. You've been let down so many times, that's all you expect. I'd hoped I could change that for you when you came to live here. Honey, things don't change in just a few years. I can't undo what your parents did to you or how Jordan made you feel. But I can love you, and I do. I can be patient with you, and I am. I can promise to be there for you every day of my life, and I will. It's all I have, and I hope one day you'll accept it."

"Oh, Charlie," I whisper. I want to keep crying, but I can't. I have no tears left.

"Now, will you help me lay Viola to rest?" He takes my hand so that we stand together, then picks up the urn and removes the lid. His hand disappears in the ceramic mouth, and then comes out grasping a handful of ash. We take turns pulling out ash and flinging it into the air. The wind carries Viola's ash across the bare vineyards, spreading them throughout the land they had bought years ago, when all they had was a dream. Now, they'd built a legacy.

And I get to be part of it.

That evening, Charlie throws me an official welcome home party. Jace and his family are the first to arrive. I'm shy as Jace hugs me hello. It's different now. I feel like I've woken up from a bad dream. I'm embarrassed Jace saw me in such a vulnerable state. More than that, I'm grateful. He and his family saved me. Because of them, I feel human again, like I have a chance at a normal life.

The farmhands arrive with their wives and children. Fátima's brothers are there, too. Fátima spoils us all with a feast of tamales, pozole, a taco bar, and every other dish I missed while I was gone. I overfill my plate, and notice I'm not alone. Thankfully, she made enough food to feed the neighborhood.

I'm relieved no one asks me to talk about the time I was away. I have a feeling Charlie and Fátima warned people to avoid the subject. Instead, we talk about how much Hope has grown, my plans for the near future, how skinny I am. I lost thirty pounds since June, though I'm certain Fátima will do her best to put the weight back on. Tonight is a good start, and I eat until I can eat no more, but still find room for dessert. By the time everyone starts to leave, I'm full in my belly and heart.

Jace stays when his family leaves. He brought his car so he could spend more time with me. We put Hope to bed, and begin helping Fátima and a few of the wives clean up, but they shoo us out of the kitchen. Charlie says goodnight, and I catch the wink he gives Jace as he turns the corner.

"Want to go for a drive?" Jace asks. We bundle up before we head out into the winter night air. He cranks up the car heater. I rub my hands together as the car warms up, and he takes them and blows hot air on them. His lips against my fingers send a shiver through me, and he grins when he notices. He turns the radio on, and Coldplay croons softly from the speakers. My hand is back in his as we drive.

Part of me wants to hold his hand tightly and never let go. But I also want to push him away and save him from my brokenness. I fight that feeling, and weave my fingers through his. His warm skin keeps me grounded, and I pretend I'm normal enough to deserve someone as kind and patient as Jace.

We drive through town, and then onto the back roads toward Bodega Bay. The moon is full tonight, and I watch it as we make the winding trek through the hills. I think back to a month before, staring at the full moon as I made the biggest decision of my life. It feels like a lifetime ago. When I think of our life in Oregon, it's almost like I'm looking down on someone else's life. I want to forget everything. At the same time, I want to remember all of it.

We turn the corner and the ocean spreads out in front of us. Jace pulls into an empty parking lot on a bluff over the ocean. He turns the car off, and the music is replaced by waves crashing below us. He puts his hand back in mine, but doesn't speak. Neither of us do. We just look at the ocean, lit by the moon's reflection. I feel small next to this huge expanse of water. My fears feel small. Jordan, my life in Oregon, this moment—it's all small in the grand scheme of things. Everything that wants to shut me down, stifle my voice, and beat me into submission is nothing compared to the endless sea. Despite the dropping temperature inside the car, I feel a sense of warmth as I shrink and the ocean expands. I'm safe now, surrounded by love from people who are rallying around me. Jace. Charlie. Fátima. Grace and Tom. Everyone who showed up tonight to welcome me home. Charlie called me the prodigal daughter, and I remember the Bible story I'd heard as a kid. In it, a son had taken an early inheritance from his father and ended up losing it in a series of bad decisions. When he had nowhere else to turn, he came back home, meaning to offer himself as his father's servant. Instead, his father welcomed him with open arms, and threw a feast to celebrate his son's return. When his other son asked about this, the father said there was reason to celebrate, as his son was lost and now was found.

Charlie forgave me when I couldn't forgive myself. He loved me even when I thought I was unlovable. I'd never known love like this. Jordan and my parents—the people I'd placed the most trust in—they'd all let me down. But Charlie stuck by me, even though I pushed him away. He showed me what real love looks like.

So did Jace.

I look at him, studying his face as he watches the sea. He doesn't owe me anything. The first time I pushed him away should have been the last. When I moved on with Jordan, he should have disappeared. When I called him to rescue me, he shouldn't have picked up. When I withered away in his living room, he should have been disgusted. But he wasn't. He never looked at me as if I were less. He stayed by my side as much as I'd let him.

"I don't deserve you." The words reach my lips before my mind can tell me to stay silent. Jace touches my face.

"Yes you do, and so much more."

I don't speak, the tears burning in my eyes. I'm tired of crying and feeling sorry for myself. But dang, it's hard to keep my emotions inside when he's looking at me this way—like I'm someone special.

I'm damaged goods. I want to pull away and tell him to take me home. He shouldn't be around someone like me. He's so good and so kind, and I'm dirty around the edges. He offered me the world, and I pushed him away for someone who treated me terribly. If I stay, I run the risk of allowing my baggage to ruin how good he is.

But then there's the way he's looking at me. It's as if he can't see all my dirty edges, as if I never hurt him. The recent past evaporates. I feel worthy and whole, beautiful, loved.

"Come here," he whispers, and he pulls me to him. I let him, choosing to let go of my inhibitions and reservations, and accept everything he's been trying to give me all along. His lips touch mine, and I whimper as I give in. He touches my face as his kiss deepens. I grasp his shirt, pulling him closer. Finally, I'm free.

"Thank you," I say when our lips part. I love the way his cheek creases as he smiles. Why did I let him go? How could I not see that he was everything Hope and I needed?

"For what?" My hand is still in his, and I love how protected and safe it makes me feel.

"For not giving up on me."

"I've never given up on you. I couldn't. I lo…" He stops, then gives an embarrassed laugh.

"You, what?" My heart is racing as I realize what he stopped himself from saying.

"Nothing." He starts to pull his hand away, but I hold on tight.

"Please, tell me," I beg him. He winces, but then relaxes into a smile.

"I love you," he says. I open my mouth to speak, but he shakes his head. "Don't say anything. Just hear me out. I know it's too soon to say anything like that. After what you've been through, it's probably asking you a lot just to let me get close to you now. He hurt you in ways I'll never understand, and you need time to heal. But I love you, Maddie. I do. I've loved you since the first day I saw you in that coffee shop, when that barista dude dismissed you just because you had a child. I loved you when I saw you standing in front of me with a pee stain on your shirt. I loved you when I kissed you for the first time, and when you broke my heart. I loved you every time you texted me back, and every day you were gone. I loved you when you called me to save you. I loved you every day you lay on my couch. I wanted to curl up with you, take away your pain, heal your heart, and absorb your burdens. I wanted to tell you every day I saw you that I loved you, that I've always loved you, and I always *will* love you. I don't even care if you can't tell me you love me back. In fact, *don't* say it. Not yet. But I can't go another day without letting you know how deeply in love with you I am, and that I will never, ever let you go."

He holds my gaze for a few seconds more, then glances at our hands. I move my hand to his chin so he'll keep looking at me, the words I'm about to say already in my heart.

"I love you, too." I see his shoulders lower and relief cross his face. "I loved you back then, but I was afraid. You were everything I wanted, but I was afraid I was asking too much of you. You're too young to be a father." He starts to argue with me, but it's my turn to keep him from talking. "I know you don't feel that way, but it's how I felt. That's why I broke things off with you, not because I didn't care for you but because I cared so much. I didn't want to burden you with raising my daughter when you had your own live to live." I take a deep breath, then continue. "I met Jordan again the day I broke up with you. If I'd told him to get lost like I wanted to, everything would be so different now. You would have talked some sense into me. I wouldn't have experienced the awfulness Jordan put me through. I'd be in college, maybe have a better idea of what I want to do with my life. Everything would be so much better. But I didn't. I chose Jordan because I thought that was the right choice. He's Hope's dad, and he said he was interested in making a life with her. I felt I needed to give him that chance, ignoring every time he'd let me down. It didn't take long for me to remember."

I pause, and Jace starts to say something, but I stop him. "There's something I need to tell you. I thought of you every day, especially when Jordan began hitting me. I wanted to call you, have you help me get out of there. But I felt like if I did, I'd only be dragging you into a mess that wasn't yours. I was worried about your safety, and that my feelings were clouded again. I felt like if I called you, I'd only be running to you because I was running away from Jordan. I couldn't see up from down, and didn't know what my true feelings were."

"What changed your mind?" Jace asks.

"I was desperate. I had no one to turn to, and I knew you'd be there. I knew even if you were angry with me, you'd be there."

"So, not because you loved me," he says.

"I always loved you. But then, I didn't know *what* I felt. I was afraid of opening myself up to anyone, especially you, after the way he hurt me. I knew you'd never hurt me that way, but I was so broken I was afraid I'd make you as toxic as I was. But that's the thing. You came and brought me home. You took care of me when I couldn't take care of myself. You gave me a safe place to grieve and come to terms with everything I've been through. I'm not done yet, but you set me on a path of healing. You stuck by me at my worst. I mean, you saw me when I hadn't showered or brushed my teeth in days, and you still looked at me like I was beautiful."

"I'll always think you're beautiful."

"And that's why I love you. You see straight through me, the good parts and the ugly parts, and you accept me as I am and make me feel beautiful. I've never known anyone like you, and I want to be loved by you for the rest of my life. I know it's too soon for either of us to be saying 'I love you,' but I don't care. I want to say it every time I'm around you, and I never want anything to stand in our way again."

"I love you, Maddie," Jace breathes, pulling me to him again.

"Say it again," I whisper.

"I love you." Then he presses his lips to mine.

Judgement

I'm shaking as I stand outside the courtroom. Jace squeezes my hand and I look at him.

"It's going to be okay," he promises, but he can't know that. I've done everything I can. I even included the photos Jace took of my injuries with the statement I gave the police. They're proof I'm not lying, and I'm grateful he insisted on taking the photos. But the decision on Hope's custody is out of my hands. In the past few weeks, I'd felt confident they were enough. Now, I'm not so sure. The judge must see fifteen, maybe twenty custody cases a day. He might not believe me, or think I'm trying to pull strings to get full custody. It's a crazy thought, since the photos prove Jordan abused me. But the photos might not be enough. I have visual evidence, but Jordan has a way with words. If anyone can talk someone out of seeing the truth, it's him.

And suddenly, he's there. My heart is racing as I look at him for the first time in almost two months. His tattoos are mostly hidden under a suit and tie, his face clean-shaven, and his hair slicked back. To a stranger, he probably looks clean cut, even trustworthy. To me, he's more terrifying than ever. I don't know what to expect.

I shiver as he stares straight at me. Charlie's standing behind me. He puts his hand on my shoulder, but all I see is Jordan. I know he can't do anything to me here. We're surrounded by people, and I'm flanked by two men who will die before letting him get to me. It doesn't matter. When he sneers at me, I turn away. I can't stop shaking. I feel sick to my stomach. This day can't be over soon enough.

"He can't touch you," Jace says, standing in front of me so I'm blocked from Jordan's view. I'm not afraid of him hurting me physically, but what he'll say about me, and what the court will believe after he's lied about me. More than that, I'm scared of what he's thinking of me. It feels wrong to worry about that, but this is a man who once told me he loved me. I'd been so wrong about him, and I feel like the truth is cutting me in two. Everything I went through in Oregon comes back now that we're in the same room. I've had a month to be free from the past, to forget and heal—from doctor's visits to check for fractures (my nose wasn't broken, thankfully), to counseling visits to help heal my heart. But now, the abuse, his words, the darkness, my depression—they consume me and I can't breathe.

"I need to get out of here," I whisper, but the courtroom door opens and people file in. The air seems thinner, and I'm hot and cold. I no longer want to do this, but I have to if I want to keep my daughter safe. I focus on her, remembering the moment in Oregon when she said she was going to tell her daddy I smiled at Ashton. I have to be strong for her, or she'll believe it's okay for a woman to be property. If I walk out now, everything I've done for her won't matter. I'll never be safe, and she'll be influenced by the wrong kind of role model.

"I'll be here the whole time," Jace promises, taking my hand as we join the end of the line. The three of us sit in the same row as Jordan, but on the opposite side of the court. I'm shaken by being so close to him, but glad I can't see him. Charlie and Jordan sit on either side of me. I'm grateful they're here, but they can't protect me from what I feel.

We rise as the judge enters, then sit when he tells us. He already appears tired. He puts on a pair of glasses, then explains how this is a court that looks for the child's best interests. For fifteen minutes, he scolds us in a way that makes me feel wrong for even being here. But I'm here for the right reasons. I'm sure of it. *I am, right?*

The judge calls up the first case, and a blonde woman comes forward and sits at the table facing the judge, joined by two men on other side. One of the men is the lawyer of the other man, but the woman has no lawyer. I listen to the case with interest and clenched hands, trying to follow the court process, and what I can expect. Charlie had offered to get me a lawyer, but I insisted I didn't need one. I didn't want to spend more of his money, and I knew Jordan wouldn't have one. I figured this case would be easy—Jordan was abusive, I had a restraining order, Hope wasn't safe in any kind of environment he provided, and I'd turned my life around to make sure she was cared for properly. It's a no-brainer. But now, I wonder if I made a mistake. This feeling grows as the first case unfolds.

The woman tells her side of the story—how her husband cheated on her throughout their marriage and is now harassing her by lying about her to family and friends. She shares what it's like when he gets the kids, how they don't want to go to his house because he beats them with a belt. She paints a picture of a man who left the parenting up to her, and who's only fighting her so he doesn't have to pay too much child support. She requests a split custody agreement, with the kids seeing their father every other weekend.

When it's the man's turn, his lawyer speaks for him. He doesn't mention anything about the marriage, but tells how the man recently moved into a home with a bedroom for each child. He describes how the man works around his kids' schedules so they have more quality time together. He shares the number of times his client paid for the kids' clothing and school items, and has receipts to prove the payments. He tells about the routine at his client's house, and how the kids are still adjusting, but it seems they're doing well. Then, sounding troubled, the lawyer mentions the anti-depressants the woman is taking, and questions her ability to care for the kids.

"For the safety of their children, my client requests full custody with no visitation until the defendant undergoes a full psychiatric analysis," the lawyer says. He sits back in his chair with a concerned look. In contrast, I notice the man's smug expression, and the horrified look on his ex-wife's face. I want her to speak up, tell the judge why she's taking anti-depressants, and seek full custody. I hold my breath, silently pleading with her to keep fighting.

The judge flips through the report in front of him before making his ruling. No one speaks, and there's no noise except for the judge's shuffling papers. Then he looks at the people in front of him.

I want to crawl out of my skin as he reads the verdict—a 50/50 split, with the children staying in each parent's home every other week. Since their incomes are close to equal, the man is ordered to pay only $125 in child support.

I can tell the woman is trying not to cry as the bailiff directs her to where she needs to wait for her paperwork. Then my name and Jordan's are called.

It's too soon. I haven't had time to process what I just saw. I've forgotten every defense I had.

I let go of Jace's hand and make my way to the table in front of the judge. I don't look at Jordan or the judge as we take our seats. I'm so nervous, I feel like I could throw up.

The judge announces the nature of our case, mentioning the meeting each of us had with a mediator the week before, saying that the mediator suggests awarding full custody to me, and visitation for Jordan. I look up to see how Jordan reacts. His face is stone, but his eyes narrow.

"Ms. Russo, I'll hear from you first." I take a few deep breaths before I begin. I want to tell him everything, from the day I left my parents' house to the last beating, but I know it will make me look weak and emotional. I think of the case before ours, how the man and his lawyer didn't give much information about life before the divorce, but focused on what he could do now.

"I've been Hope's primary guardian since the day she was born," I begin. "We live on a vineyard in a large house with Dad....with Mr. Winston. We've been there three years, with only a short time in between when Jordan and I lived in Oregon. Hope has her own room. All her toys are there, and all her needs are met. I'm about to start college to take classes in viticulture and business so I can learn more about running a winery. Everything I've done has been to give Hope a better life. Jordan, on the other hand, can't promise that. He wasn't in her life the first two years. I don't know where he's living now, but none of his most recent arrangements have been places to raise a child. He wouldn't know what to do if she got sick because that's always been my job. His primary concern is not taking care of a toddler, it's taking care of himself. Because I can provide a more stable environment for her, I ask for what the mediator recommends—full custody with weekly visitation."

I'm not confident about anything I've just said. I regret not mentioning the abuse, but I know the judge can see it right in front of him.

"Mr. Turner." The judge turns to Jordan. "The court will hear from you now."

"Sure. But first, Ms. Russo is lying," Jordan says. I jerk my head in his direction and catch his smirk. He doesn't look at me, but continues addressing the judge. "Maddie was arrested when she was still pregnant with Hope for trying to steal a woman's purse. I didn't know she was like that when it happened. She was arrested before I could do anything, and her parents bailed her out. When she finally got out, she ran. I couldn't find her, and neither could her parents. She ended up sleeping on the streets, probably selling her body to get money. She was still living on the streets when she had Hope, and tried to give our daughter up so she could continue her way of living. If it weren't for the Winstons, she would have succeeded. Luckily they talked some sense into her and she ended up keeping Hope."

"You lying sack of shit," I hear Charlie bellow. I'm already furious at the way Jordan's twisted the truth. I turn to see Charlie standing up, his face red as he glares at Jordan.

"Order!" the judge commands. "Sir, sit down. One more outburst and I'll have you escorted out of the courtroom."

"Your Honor," I say, but the judge holds up a finger.

"You'll have a chance for rebuttal in a moment. Right now, it's Mr. Turner's time to speak."

Jordan continues lying to the judge, saying that I hid from him to keep him from our daughter.

"If I hadn't seen Maddie in a café, I never would have known Hope at all," Jordan says, his voice shaking. He tells the judge about our relationship, how we made up and rekindled what we had before. "But Your Honor, it was all about Hope. I'm sorry to say I never loved Maddie, but I knew I'd never get to know my daughter if I didn't pretend to love her. I figured time might change my feelings, especially when we moved to Oregon so we could be a family. Unfortunately, this never happened. I worked full time, and she used that as an opportunity to mess around with other guys. She'd leave Hope with strangers so she could go out while I was gone. She refused to get a job, and there were times we ran out of food because she wouldn't go shopping. She ended up meeting the wrong guy while we were there, and he knocked her around. That's when she left, probably afraid I'd find out. Thing is, Your Honor, I knew the whole time. I just didn't want to risk losing Hope."

"So these photos I have in front of me," the judge says, gesturing to his desk. "These injuries came from this other man, and not you?"

"That's correct, Your Honor," Jordan says. I clench my hands as I wait for my turn to speak. I'm both furious and petrified. What if the judge believes him? It seems impossible, but I've been wrong so many times before.

"Ms. Russo says you may not have a place to live, Mr. Turner. Is that correct? And…" The judge looks down at his paperwork again. "It says here that you don't have any income. Is that also true?"

"Yes, Your Honor," Jordan says. "I mean, to both of those. I'm living with a friend right now, but there's room for Hope to stay. I haven't started working yet, but I have a job lined up at my buddy's construction company. I'll be working five days a week, and will have enough to support Hope."

"It says here that you're fighting for full custody," the judge said. Jordan nodded.

"Yes. At this time, I don't feel that it's right for Hope to stay with a woman who didn't want her, and who continues to put our daughter last while she serves her own selfish needs. I mean," he smirks toward Jace and Charlie, "she even brought a date to a court hearing."

Everything he's saying is a lie. But the judge doesn't know me. I'm the only one who knows my side of the story. Well, me, Charlie, and Jace. Everyone in this courtroom could believe what Jordan is saying. They could think I'm the liar, not him.

"Ms. Russo?"

I look up. The judge is staring at me.

"I'm sorry, what?" I ask. Jordan snorts next to me.

"I asked, did you have anything to add before I rule?"

Jordan's expression says he's already won. I don't think I can hate him any more than I do right now. He's so sure of himself, so cocky. I'm recovering from the worst six months of my life, and he's acting as if none of it happened. He put me through hell, and then has the audacity to make it seem like I'm the unfit parent. He owes me. He *owes me*.

I nod. I know what I need to say. And so I do. I start with the day I told my parents I was pregnant with Hope, and how they threw me out. I tell him how I moved in with Jordan and his parents, and how his dad almost raped me. I talk about our drive to San Francisco, how Jordan stole a man's wallet, and how the money was what we lived on for the next few weeks. I share about moving in with Ben and Jill, and how Jordan stole their money, too, before we took off up the coast. I tell him how we ended up in Petaluma, and how he talked me into stealing a wallet.

"I didn't think I had any other choice," I say to the judge. "We had no money and nowhere to go, and somehow he made it sound like it was a good idea. Looking back, I should have said no. I should have tried to find a job on my own and learned how to support myself. I should have left him a long time ago, but I didn't know how. I thought he loved me, and I thought I loved him, too. I was scared and alone. But it wasn't until I was arrested and he took off that I learned what being alone was really like."

I know I'm saying too much. This is more than what the judge is asking for, and I know I'm taking up a lot of the court's time. But I'll talk until the judge tells me I can't anymore, and since he isn't stopping me, I go on. I tell him about the nights I spent sleeping in that parking lot, and the days I went hungry. And then I share about Charlie and Viola.

"They saved me, and they continued to save me every day." I tell him about working for them, and the money I set aside to give Hope the life she deserves. And then I admit the doubts I had when I held her for the first time. "I was still homeless, sir, and didn't know if I'd be able to take care of her. Sleeping on the streets was one thing for me, but it's no place to raise a baby. I knew there was a family out there who could take care of her in a way I couldn't. So I tried to give her up. Thankfully, Charlie and Viola offered me a place in their home, and a chance to be Hope's mother."

I feel ashamed as I talk about things I've kept hidden, especially from Jace. I wonder how he's reacting, but I can't stop now. I have to keep going, for my daughter's sake. All of this is for Hope.

I tell the judge about my life after moving in with the Winstons, how I graduated high school while raising a baby, and how I learned to work on the farm so that one day I could be part of the business. I tell the judge how everything I've done has been with Hope in mind, how I want to make a better future for us so that she doesn't have the kind of life I escaped. Then I tell him about running into Jordan.

"When I first saw him, I was so angry. He'd left me to care for Hope on my own. He was more worried about his freedom than us. When he saw I was being arrested for something we both were involved in, he took off and never looked back."

"I searched for you!" Jordan cut in.

"No, you didn't," I said. "You can't even keep your lies straight. You already admitted you didn't look for me, that you were scared. Besides, I was there every day and every night. I watched for you, and would have seen you if you'd been there. You never came back to find me."

I turn back to the judge. "Jordan and I did get back together. We began seeing each other in secret, but I eventually told Charlie what was going on. He was supportive of my decisions, but didn't approve. He was right, of course."

I push past my shame and share the rest of my story. I tell him about the first sign of violence I saw from Jordan, when he broke my phone and grabbed my wrist. I tell him about moving to a pot farm, and about the abuse that went on for months. I tell him how Jordan left us alone for days at a time, and about the time we ran out of food. I tell him how Jordan accused me of cheating on him so that I couldn't even look at anyone, afraid he'd get the wrong idea.

"I left him on the night of my birthday. I'd been alone for days. One of the guys found out it was my birthday, and made sure Hope and I were taken care of. It was nothing more than a friendly gesture, but Jordan came home and thought it was something more. He beat me, and then he raped me. After that, he drank so much he passed out. That was when we escaped. Those pictures you have in front of you are after Jordan beat me on my birthday. *He* did that to me, not someone else."

I pause, taking a deep breath, searching for my courage before I continue. "Your Honor, I want to change my custody request. I ask for full legal and physical custody with no visitation by Mr. Turner. Our daughter is not safe in his presence. If he's granted any custody, I know it's only a matter of time before he abuses her like he abused me."

"You fucking twat!" Jordan roars as he stands. The bailiff rushes forward and places himself between us before Jordan can touch me.

"Sit down, Mr. Turner," the judge orders.

"She's lying!" he shouts, still not sitting. "I would never hurt my daughter."

"Mr. Turner, sit down or I will hold you in contempt of court."

Jordan sits, but the bailiff remains between us.

The judge regards us for a moment.

"In the case of Russo vs. Turner, I rule that—"

"Don't I get a rebuttal to her rebuttal?" Jordan cuts in.

"What is your rebuttal?" the judge asks.

"That Maddie is lying, and should be the one held in contempt of court."

"Is that all?"

Jordan leans back in his chair, and then looks at me around the bailiff between us.

"Yeah, that's all." He doesn't need to say anything else. The look he gives me brings back to every moment just before he laid hands on me; it's the one that warned me I was moments away from trouble and he was about to teach me a lesson. I refuse to shrink down in my seat, to appear weak. Instead, I face forward and hold my head high.

"In the case of Russo vs. Turner, I grant full legal and physical custody to Madeline Russo, with supervised visitation to Jordan Turner once a week. The restraining order will stay in place for twelve months, with the only contact occurring at the weekly supervised visitation."

"This is bullshit!" Jordan shouts.

"Further, Jordan Turner is to attend court-ordered anger management classes, along with parenting classes for twelve months," the judge continues. He looks at Jordan. "This case will be revisited in one year's time. However, if you still feel the need to use obscenities in my court, we can make this order stand two years."

"No, Your Honor," Jordan says through his teeth.

"Finally, Mr. Turner is to pay Ms. Russo $425 per month for child support."

"But—"

"I know you don't have a job right now," the judge interrupts. "But you are capable of holding a job, and I suggest you get one soon."

I refuse to look at Jordan again when I join Charlie and Jace. I try to keep my face calm, but know my joy is obvious—mostly because I can see it in Charlie and Jace's eyes. I sign the papers the bailiff hands me, and wait for him to bring me my copy. Once it's in my hand, we're free to go.

In the hallway, we finally relax. I hadn't realized how tense I'd been. It feels like a huge weight has been lifted off me.

"You were brilliant," Jace says, giving me a kiss on the cheek.

"I was terrified," I admit.

We turn the corner, and Jordan is there. I can tell he's been waiting for us. He's leaning against the wall, but stands straight when he sees me.

"You'll pay for this, bitch," he hisses.

"Wait here," Charlie says. He steps toward Jordan. "I've had enough of you," Charlie tells him. Jordan's jaw is set, and I move closer to Jace. If Jordan could hit me, he'd have no problem going after Charlie.

"What will you do about it, old man?" Jordan taunts him.

"At this moment, not a damn thing. You see, we have a court order here that says you can't be within 300 feet of Maddie or Hope, and you are violating that order. All I have to do is go to the closest bailiff, and we can have you arrested."

Jordan makes no move to back off.

"I realize that once we leave this court, a piece of paper may not offer all the protection we need if you decide to violate the order again. If that's the case, I think you should know that I keep a rifle close by in case any intruders trespass on my property."

"Is that a threat?" Jordan asks.

"No, that's just information I'm passing along." Charlie turns back to me. "Come on, let's go home." He gives me a secret smile, and I return it. Then the three of us leave the courthouse so we can finally move on with our lives.

Fear

I love kissing Jace. His lips are soft and warm, and his scent is intoxicating. He never seeks more than my mouth when he's kissing me, allowing me to feel innocent again, even though our desire lies underneath. We savor this feeling, not wanting to rush through our firsts. I know it will be exciting the first time we make love, but I'm not ready to go there yet. If this frustrates him, he doesn't let me know.

His lips break from mine, and he smiles while stroking the side of my cheek.

"You were incredible today," he says.

"I just showed up." I'm relieved I won't have to be in court for another year, though I wish I didn't have to let Hope see her father ever again. She has a right to know her father, and I know Jordan loves her, but I hate that he'll still be an influence for her. He won't be her only role model, though, and I hope she'll recognize the difference between Jordan and men like Charlie and Jace. I hope it's enough, that she'll grow up believing a good man is someone who respects her, cherishes her, and helps bring out the best in her.

"You did more than show up," Jace argues. "You laid it all out on the table. That couldn't have been easy."

"It wasn't," I admit. "I thought the judge wanted to hear about what we were doing now to give Hope the best life possible. But when Jordan lied about me, I realized I wasn't fighting hard enough. The judge didn't know what life was like with Jordan. I had to make him understand."

"It worked." Jace leans in to me to kiss me again, but I turn my head. "What's up?" he asks.

"I said a lot of things today you didn't know about me. Did any of that…did it surprise you?"

"I knew things were rough for you, but I never knew you were homeless, or that you almost gave up Hope."

"Does that change your feelings for me?"

He took my hands in his. "Look at me." I did, and softened under his gaze. "I can't imagine what you went through back then. You must have been so scared and alone. What you did for Hope, though, was completely selfless. You thought of her first."

"But what if Charlie and Viola hadn't taken me in? I would have lost Hope forever!"

"And she would have lived a happy, safe life," he says. "She wouldn't have known you, but she also wouldn't have known the hardships you knew." He squeezes my hand. "You put her life before yours, and everything worked out in the end."

"Yeah, after I totally screwed everything up. I never should have left with Jordan."

"Do you really think you can protect Hope from every bad thing in life?" he asks. I shake my head, but then I nod. He laughs. "Which is it?"

"I'm trying to protect her," I say. "But I've made so many bad decisions that have hurt her."

"You're human. You're not perfect. But from where I sit, you're doing a hell of a job with what life has thrown at you. I think you should be proud of yourself and what you've bounced back from. You're an incredible woman. I wish you could see that."

The front porch light is the only light on when we get back, meaning Charlie's gone to bed. Jace kisses me at the door, and I lean against him.

"I hate missing you when you leave," I say.

"Well, maybe one day you won't have to." It's another reference to our future, and my stomach fills with butterflies...the good kind. A life with Jace would be easy. It would be wonderful, everything I've dreamed of. But we won't rush. Right now, it's all about small steps forward and healing.

I wait by the door until I can't see his taillights on the road. Then I head inside. Before I go to my room, I check on Hope. Her door creaks, and I hope she won't wake up. I can see from the hall light that her breathing is even. It's been a week since we got her a toddler bed, one she miraculously stays in. I think it helps that it's Disney-themed, with Elsa and Anna from the movie, *Frozen,* on it, covered with a canopy. It's the kind of princess bed I wanted when I was a little girl—a frivolous bed my military father would have shut down if I'd dared to ask him for it. It's why I didn't say no when Hope pointed it out and when Charlie insisted on buying it. Because of Charlie, she'd have the childhood she deserved.

"Because of me, too," I whisper. I'm not there yet. I have to get an education first, and moving forward won't be an overnight journey. But now, I'm determined nothing will stand in my way. I'm doing this for her—and for me. "I'll make you so proud of me," I promise her. "Everything will be different now, you'll see."

I memorize her rosy cheeks and the way her hair curls around her face, just as I do every time I look at her. Each day she seems further away from the pudgy baby I used to hold. Now she's this little being with her own thoughts and feelings. Soon she'll start school, go on playdates, make friends, become more independent... I want it all for her, and I want to always be there to cheer her on. I've never loved anyone as much as I love her, and I hope I always do right by her. I can't think of anything she could do that would make me turn my back on her. Even if she came home pregnant as a teenager, I'd take her in my arms and tell her we'll figure it out together, because that's what parents do—they love their children no matter what.

I brush my lips against her cheek, then tiptoe back to my room and shut the door. I run the bathwater and strip out of my clothes while the tub fills. I play Coldplay quietly on the new phone Charlie gave me, setting it near the tub. It makes me think of the night Jace and I drove out to the beach and shared our second first kiss. My phone beeps as I'm about to lean back in the tub, and I reach for it.

Jace: *Home safe. I love you.*

Me: *I love you, too. Sleep well.*

I set the phone down and relax in the water. Coldplay continues, telling me that everything's not lost. I stay in the water until my fingers and toes look like prunes, then dry off and slip on a robe. Phone in hand, I open the door and a cloud of steam enters my cool bedroom.

"I thought you should say goodbye to your daughter."

"Jordan," I gasp, moving to take Hope from him. That's when he shows me the gun he's hiding behind her back. She's smiling, touching his face as he places the gun against her again. She has no idea.

"Mama, Daddy's here!" she exclaims. Jordan smiles at her. I take a chance and touch Jace's name from our texts so the phone will call him.

"That's right, baby girl. And no one is ever taking you away from me again."

I slip the phone behind my back and place it face down on my nightstand before Jordan looks at me again. I only hope that Jace hears enough of our conversation to know to call the police.

As Jordan looks at me, the smile is still on his face, but his eyes are full of rage. "Don't scream," he warns me. "And don't think of stopping me or I'll pull the trigger. I'll kill her, and it will be all your fault."

"You'd kill your own daughter?" I'm shaking, but keep my voice even so he doesn't know how scared I am.

"If I can't have her, neither will you."

"Then you don't love her," I say. He glares at me, and moves the gun from Hope's back and points it at me. Even after everything we've been through, I don't think he has it in him to commit murder. I hope I'm not wrong.

"Don't tell me who I love or don't love," he hisses. "I love Hope more than you could ever know."

"You mean, the way I've loved her every day of her life?" I ask him.

"No! You tried to give her up!"

"Because I loved her so much! I had nothing for her. I was sleeping on a pile of clothes in a parking lot. I couldn't let her to grow up that way. I had to give her up if I wanted her to live a good life. Don't you want her to have a good life?"

"Yes! But you want to take her away from me."

He lowers the gun, and his expression softens. I realize I might be able to get through to him. If I act cool and pretend nothing is wrong, maybe I can get him to put her down.

"I don't want you out of her life," I say. I sit down on the bed, relaxing my stance in hopes that he will, too. "I think Hope should have both of us in her life. We're not meant to be together, but that doesn't mean we can't both be her parents."

"Yeah, but now I'm only allowed to see her once a week while some person watches my every move. It's not fair. I fell in love with her, and now you want to take her away from me."

He wants to talk fairness. He hurt me repeatedly, right in front of our daughter.

"Let's work this out, then," I tell him. "We can forget the court order and do things our way." I watch him carefully, seeing the tender way he looks at her. I think he's thinking things over, but then he looks back at me with hardened eyes.

"I don't believe you."

"Jordan, seriously. What do you want? I'll do it. Just let me know."

He continues to glare at me. He adjusts Hope in his arms, and I hold my breath as he moves the gun to her back again, but this time casually as if it's an extension of his hand. One wrong move… I shudder and try not to think about it. I need to focus. I need *him* to focus.

"Tell me. Let's figure this out together, okay?" He backs up toward the door, and I feel panic inside me. "Jordan, tell me what you want!"

"I want her," he says, and then runs from the room. I grab my phone. It's off, which means it didn't call Jace after all. I dial 9-1-1 as I race after them. I hear the front door slam open before I'm in the hallway.

"Charlie!" I yell.

"9-1-1, what's your emergency?"

"He's got a gun!" I scream. "He kidnapped my daughter!" I hear Charlie running down the stairway as I go out the door. Jordan's taillights are moving down the road. I give the dispatchers the address, but it feels pointless. He's at the edge of the drive; I hear his tires squealing as he turns onto the road. I sink to my knees, dropping the phone as I watch my whole world disappear. Then I hear the crash.

"Charlie!" He's already running down the road.

"Stay there!" he calls, but I don't listen. I'm up and running again. I barely feel the gravel cutting into my bare feet and the cool air penetrating my skin under my flimsy robe. All I want is my daughter.

My lungs are aching when we reach the end of the drive. Jordan's car is turned in the opposite direction on the road, its side crushed against a post and a falling down fence.

"Oh my God," I whisper. I know Jordan couldn't have put Hope in a car seat. I hear sirens in the distance as I move toward the car.

"Maddie, keep back," Charlie orders as he points his rifle toward the car.

"My baby." My tears blur my vision and my heart hurts. "Please let her be okay." I see movement in the car. Jordan opens the door. "Give me my daughter!" I scream. He's holding her as he steps out of the car. I'm relieved to see her alive. She's crying, a good sign. The sirens are deafening as the police cars round the corner and surround us.

"Sir, drop your weapon," a voice says over the intercom. Charlie puts his hands in the air, and then slowly places his rifle on the ground. An officer steps toward him and places Charlie's hands behind his back.

"It's not him!" I scream, pointing at Jordan, my eyes glued on the gun he's holding against Hope. "That's him! He's trying to take my daughter!" He has a gash on his forehead, but as far as I can tell, Hope seems unhurt. "Jordan, please put her down," I plead. Hope continues to wail, trying to push herself away from him. He keeps a tight hold on her, and presses the gun against her head.

"Don't come near me," he warns, shifting his eyes from me to the police, their guns trained on him.

"Sir, put the gun down," one of the cops says. "We don't want anyone to get hurt."

Jordan turns back to me.

"Jordan, please. You're scaring her." He appears blurry in front of me as the tears continue to fall. "Just put her down. We can work this out, okay?"

"Don't you see? We can't! *You* did this, Maddie. You're *making* me do this!" He keeps the gun at her head, and I'm afraid he'll really shoot her. I see a cop creeping closer, but he stops when Jordan looks in his direction. "I'll shoot," he threatens. "Don't test me, I'll do it."

"Sir, is this your daughter?" the cop asks. Jordan stares at him for a few seconds, then gives a slight nod. Hope is still crying, but isn't struggling to get away anymore. My heart breaks for her. "What's your name, sir?" the cop asks.

"What does it matter?" Jordan growls.

"My name's Officer Paul Chretien, but you can call me Paul, okay? What's your name?"

"Jordan," he whispers.

"Okay, Jordan, I'm going to lower my weapon. But my friends here, they're not, okay? I just want to talk with you man to man. Is that all right?"

Jordan nods, but doesn't say anything. He still looks angry, but that nod gives me hope. *Please God. I'll do anything. Please get through to him.*

"Now, Jordan, I want you to look at your little girl, okay? She looks kind of like you, huh?"

I see a slight smile on Jordan's face as he looks down at Hope. I'm holding my breath as I watch.

"Take a good look at her, Jordan. Do you see how scared she is?"

Jordan still has the gun against her head, but his hand wavers.

"You're her daddy, Jordan, and you're scaring her. Daddies are supposed to protect their little girls, not scare them."

I watch as Jordan's face crumples. He lowers the gun, but keeps hold of Hope.

"I know you love your little girl, Jordan. But you need to put her down. She's scared, and the best thing you can do is to put her down. Do you understand what I'm saying?"

Jordan presses his forehead against Hope's forehead. She's still crying, and now he is, too.

"Oh, baby. I'm so sorry," he whispers. He hugs her, then pulls away to look at her. "You be a good girl, okay?" His voice breaks. He kisses her forehead, and then sets her on the ground. She runs to me and I scoop her into my arms.

"Sir, put the gun down!" My heart stops as Jordan takes aim at the officer who's been talking him down. I drop to my knees, holding Hope to my chest as the officers fire. I look up in time to see Jordan falling to the ground. Charlie is on me, wrapping his arms around Hope and me. I didn't even realize I was screaming.

"It's okay," he tells me, as he holds us against him. "You're going to be okay."

Mend

The texture of my ceiling has many shapes. As I lie face up on my bed, the patches of plaster appear as drawings instead of just blotches on an otherwise smooth surface. There's the baker with his puffy white hat, a rabbit kissing the forehead of a mouse, a hammer leaning against the trunk of a tree. And there's a gun that stands alone in the middle of them all.

I often think back to the night Jordan died. Through counseling, I no longer blame myself for what happened. *I am not responsible for the choices of others.* Susan makes me repeat this at the beginning of every session. That and, *I own the things that have happened to me, but they do not define me.* For months, I wondered what I could have done differently so none of this had to happen. If I'd gone to the police the night I left him, or better, the first time he hit me. If I'd refused to leave Petaluma with him. If I'd turned and walked away when I saw him in that coffee shop. If I hadn't gone to Sausalito that day.

If I'd never met him at all.

While I know Jordan's death isn't my fault, I still feel guilt, mostly because I'm glad he's dead. Hope will never know her father, and I'm relieved. It's a terrible feeling, and one I can't talk about with anyone, not even Susan. I'll never have to hear his voice, fear his actions, resent his existence, worry what he'll do next—Hope will have this huge hole in her life, and will probably always wonder about her father. She's so young she'll forget who he was and everything about him, and I'm glad. This makes me a terrible person. Susan would disagree. She'd tell me it's a natural feeling, and totally understandable because of what I've been through. But I can't lift this burden of guilt off my shoulders. Not yet. I hated Jordan, and wanted him out of our lives forever. I never meant for him to die, and yet, his death fixes so many things in this broken life. It ends a time I'll never have to revisit again.

Except, I haven't stopped revisiting it. I'm not sure I'll ever be able to leave the past behind or when I'll stop letting it define me.

I am poverty. I am a teen mother. I am abuse. I am unworthy.

Jace has been incredible through all of this. He was there the night Jordan tried to take Hope, but I didn't know it until he walked around the police cars and reached us. My exchange with Jordan had pushed through to Jace's voicemail, and he'd heard the whole thing. He'd called the police before I dialed 9-1-1, allowing them to get there faster. If he hadn't, I don't know what would have happened. Would Jordan have gotten away? Would Charlie have shot Jordan? Would Jordan have killed us all?

Jace stayed with me that night, holding my hand as Officer Chretien took my statement. Charlie made me a cup of tea, and Jace only let go of my hand when we finally went to bed. Hope stayed in my room, and Jace slept on the couch. The next morning, he was there when memories of the night before washed over me. With time, he taught me a man could love a woman without hurting her.

Still, there are moments like this when I'm alone, and simple patches in the plaster above my head remind me of a night I wish I could forget.

Maybe I'm not supposed to forget. Maybe everything I've been through was exactly as it was supposed to be. If I hadn't met Jordan, I wouldn't have Hope. If my parents hadn't kicked me out, I wouldn't have come to Petaluma.

If I hadn't been homeless, I wouldn't have found Charlie. And if I hadn't gone to Oregon, I wouldn't have known how much I truly had.

Maybe I wasn't meant to have an easy life. I was starting to understand how hardships help us grow. I was meant to live in poverty, be a teen mom, and experience abuse. Maybe there was a bigger reason why I had to go through all of this. While these events broke me in many ways, I've become stronger through the healing process. My wounds have formed thick scar tissue. I'm more aware of the things I want in my life, and what I won't put up with. I'll never let someone mistreat my daughter or me again. I'll only trust those who deserve it. My family is now people who love and accept me. I won't be poor again because there are so many people who will catch me if I fall. I'm backing away from my identity as victim, determined to make a future for Hope and myself.

Still, I have a hard time accepting love, particularly the kind Jace wants to give me. I search the patchwork texture of my ceiling for the section that forms an almost heart. It defines my relationship with him. He offers me his heart, but I can only give him a portion of mine. I love him, but I'm afraid of letting him down. I'm also scared to let go completely. I did that with Jordan, and look where it got me.

I know it makes no sense. Jace and Jordan are completely different. While Jordan controlled me, Jace allows me to be my own person. When I was broken, he let me heal in my own time. He doesn't love me in spite of my past, but accepts me for everything I am. He gives me space when I need it, and is supportive of my hopes and dreams. I still have a hard time looking people in the eye. I'm working on it, I'm working on everything, and Jace is patient with me while I do. He knows that being with me will be an uphill climb, and he's ready to commit in every way.

I want to be ready, too. Someday, I hope I will.

I look at the time on my phone, and see a message from Jace. I hadn't heard it ping through.

Jace: *Get ready. I'll be there in 20 minutes.*

It was sent fifteen minutes ago. I shake my head with a smile.

***

He's on time, as usual. I'm late, as usual. I pack Hope's overnight bag while she tells him about the friends she's met at KinderCare. She started a few weeks ago, and it's been a godsend since I began school. I'm a semester behind, but college is college, and several months makes no difference when you're in a class of 18- to 60-year-olds. I give Charlie a kiss, and we're out the door.

We drop Hope at Jace's house, and Grace comes out as we pull into the drive.

"How's my girl?" she asks as Hope runs to her. We chat for a moment, but Jace is in a hurry to leave.

"All right, all right." I laugh as he gives his mom a look. "He won't even tell me where we're going."

"I think you'll like it," she says. She has a knowing look in her eyes, and I nudge her in protest.

"I can't believe you know before I do!"

"Honey, a mom knows everything." She looks down at Hope. "Let's go inside, KK is waiting for you." Hope doesn't even look at me after Grace sets her down. She runs to the front door and lets herself in. I knew she'd figure out doorknobs on her own.

"I'll give her a couple extra kisses tonight from you to her," Grace promises.

Jace keeps a lid on our destination the whole way there, telling me to be patient every time I try to pry it out of him. We're in the car almost two hours, with the ocean as our scenery for most of the drive. It's enough time to listen to two of Coldplay's latest albums.

"Someday we'll have to go see them in concert," I tell him. "I hear they put on an amazing show."

He finally pulls off the highway onto a steep driveway leading to office buildings.

"Wait here," he says, getting out of the car.

"You know I hate surprises."

"You like surprises," he corrects me. "You just *think* you don't."

He was right. But still…

I know we're near Mendocino, but that's all. While he's gone, I try to Google where we are so I can get a sense of what to expect, but there's no cellphone service. It's like he planned it this way.

He's back in a few minutes, jingling keys.

"Here," he says, handing me one of them. "This is a key to where we're staying, though I don't think we'll be separated the whole weekend."

"Can you at least tell me the name of the hotel?"

"There's no hotel. Stop asking questions; you'll find out soon enough."

He can't stop grinning as he drives, and I laugh at his obvious excitement. When he turns into a neighborhood, I realize why he's so excited. Each of the houses we pass is beautiful, with large bay windows facing the ocean. One is set apart from the others, and I'm elated when he pulls into the driveway.

"We're home," he says. "At least, home for the weekend."

Inside, it's better than I imagined. The other side of the house is completely glass, and the view is an endless ocean. There are no houses or pathways in front of us. We'll have complete privacy while staying here.

The kitchen is filled with food, and Jace tells me he had someone shop for us so we don't have to leave if we don't want to. The bedroom also faces west, the view perfect even when I lie on the bed. The bathroom has a Jacuzzi, and there's a hot tub on the deck. There's even an outdoor shower.

"Should we try out the hot tub?" Jace asks. I nod, suddenly shy. I'd left my swimsuit at home on purpose, knowing what this weekend would include. Up to this point, we'd kept things innocent between us. When Jace told me he wanted to take me away for a weekend, it was implied it would only happen when I wanted to take things to the next level. He made reservations as soon as I said I was ready. And I *am* ready. But now that we're here, I feel excited and nervous. Once we cross that line, there will be no going back.

I undress in the bathroom, then slip on one of the courtesy robes in the closet. When I come out, he's already undressed, a towel slung low on his hips. I haven't seen him this bare before, and my eyes travel from his face to his chest to his belly to his…

Outside, I avert my eyes when he takes off his towel and gets in the water. I wait until he isn't looking to drop my robe and join him. I know he's dying to look as I get in, just as I want to see every part of him. But I'm relieved when he gives me the time I need to settle into the hot water.

The air around us is cold and misty, but the hot water takes away the chill. My skin tingles from the contrast in temperatures. I lean my head against the side of the hot tub and look at the ocean, listening to waves that are louder than the hot tub jets. I feel Jace's hands on my shoulders, and I breathe out as he gently massages my muscles. I'm fully relaxed when he pulls me toward him so that I'm leaning against his chest. I feel every part of him behind me. This time, the butterflies are more out of anticipation than nervousness.

I don't say anything. We've had enough time for words. Instead, I turn my head so his mouth can reach mine. He places his hand in my hair and kisses me. I turn to face him, straddling his thighs. I can feel his erection, but I don't press down. I want this to last.

"Let me look at you," he says, and I stand, the cold air washing over my hot skin as his eyes travel along my body. He smiles. "You're so beautiful." He rises to meet me, and I take a step back to look at him. His shoulders and chest are broad, tapering down in a V, golden brown hair leading a trail down his chiseled abs. The muscle above his hips pulses as I take him in. He's the beautiful one.

He touches me, placing his hands on my breasts, my stomach, between my thighs. His mouth explores my skin. I shiver from his touch and the misty air.

I follow him from the tub, leaving our towels and my robe behind. He turns on the gas fireplace in our room and keeps the curtains open so that we have an uninterrupted view of the ocean. He takes his time, tasting me slowly so that I'm crawling out of my skin by the time he lifts his mouth. I move him to his back and I do the same, enjoying the way he sucks in his breath when I reach his most sensitive spots. When he can't take it anymore, he rolls over and is on top of me in one swift movement. I feel him pressing against me. I press back. His mouth is on mine as he moves against me, inside me, all around me. I am him and he is me. Everything I feared, every wall I put up, it all crumbles as he pulls my arms above my head and claims me. I never want this to end. I want every part of him to become every part of me.

We climax together. I clutch him in the final moments, tasting the salty sweat on his skin as he collapses on top of me. I have no words. I barely have breath. I hold him for a moment, feeling his chest press against me as he recovers. He lifts his head and kisses the tip of my nose, then moves to the side so he's facing me.

"Let's do that again," I say, and he laughs.

"Give me a few minutes, and that will be no problem." He keeps looking at me, and I finally avert my eyes.

"What?" I ask.

"It's just you," he says. "I could stay here forever with you. I could be with you forever. I love you, like I've never loved anyone."

I hear the promise in his voice, and despite the way he's opened me up, I can't help feeling my boundaries tug at my heart.

"I'm not ready for marriage," I blurt out. "I'm not sure I ever want to get married."

"Who said anything about marriage?" he teases, grabbing my hand under the blankets. I move closer so I can lean against him.

"I know what you're thinking," I say. "I wish I'd never been broken, because I want everything you have to give me. I want forever with you, and I want to promise that in front of everyone we know and love. If I'm ever ready, you're the one I want to be ready with. I could spend forever with you, too."

"Then let's spend forever together." He presses his mouth against my hair. When I start to protest, he shushes me. "I'm not talking marriage. I'm talking just you and me, and the simplicity of what we have right now. In this moment, I want nothing more from you. But I want nothing less, either. I just want you and me, together, forever. Is that too much to ask?"

"It sounds an awful lot like a marriage proposal." I look into his eyes, and fall in love with him all over again. His eyes, his mouth, his smile...everything about him makes me feel safe and loved. For a moment, I think I really could marry him.

"It's not a marriage proposal," he says. "You're not ready. I know that. But the thing is, I'm sure about you. I've never been more sure of anything. When I look at you, you're everything I ever dreamed I'd fall in love with. I want to fall asleep every night with your kiss on my mouth, and I want to wake up every morning and have your face be the first thing I see. I never want to let a day go by without seeing you. I want to make babies with you, go through life with you, and grow old with you. You're my best friend, and I love you."

My heart expands with his words, and I tilt my head up to meet his mouth. He presses his lips against mine for a moment before we break apart.

"I'd like that," I say. "I want every single bit of that. Please wait for me. I just want to be less broken."

"You're not broken. You're a whole person, and you're the strongest woman I know. Don't ever think you're anything less."

I take hold of his words as he presses his mouth against mine, sealing them inside as he moves on top of me and keeps his promise. What is broken, anyway? If it's not one thing that's trying to tear us apart, it's something else. I've been through hell and back. But haven't we all been through our own personal hells? Am I unworthy because I've been hurt? Does my past make me less of a person? No. I'm not broken. I'm a whole person. I'm tired of denying myself happiness just because I feel flawed from the inside out. I deserve everything Jace has to give me. I want everything he's offering.

In that moment, I know I will marry him. There's no question. Still, I make him wait six more months before I say yes.

The end.

Author's Note

Once upon a time, I met a boy who became my whole world. He was in college, and everything about him was exciting. Our romance was fast, passionate, intense. He told me he loved me within the first week and that I was unlike every other girl he'd met. So I was shocked the first time he hit me. I forgave him as soon as he apologized; I even shouldered the blame for the reason he got angry. But inside, I was screaming, knowing what he'd done was wrong, and hating myself for accepting it. I believed him when he told me it would never happen again.

Ten years later, I took off my wedding ring, packed up my children, and left, the bruises from his hands—some of many I'd hidden over the years—fading on my upper arms, my thighs, and around my neck.

I've been asked why I haven't written a memoir. *Fear.* It takes a lot of courage to write one's truth between the pages of a book, and there are some things I've pushed deep down that will be painful if I have to face them again. I'm not ready for that. Also, there is peace between my ex and me, partly because we grew up, and partly because we just don't discuss the abuse. To write a memoir would upend that peace. To write *this* may upend it.

And so, for now, I write truth in fiction. The story is pretend, but the feelings are real.

Thank you for reading the Hope series. These stories are close to my heart because a piece of me is in each character, event, and feeling.

**If you're in an abusive relationship,
there is hope, and there is help.
Visit www.thehotline.org, or call (800)799−7233.**

You do not have to live in fear.

Acknowledgements

Without the love, support, and help from several different people, this book—and series—wouldn't have been possible.

A huge thank you to my wonderful editor, Katie Watts, who polished my words and made them shine. I may not know how to use lie, lay, and laid correctly, but someday I'll get it.

A giant thank you to my children, Summer, Lucas, and Andrew, who are not really kids anymore. I lucked out being your mom/stepmom, and it's been a joy seeing you grow into young adults.

A full-hearted thank you to my parents, Nancy and Gary, who brought me in when I said the light was green, and celebrated their prodigal daughter. You were my strength when I was weak, and have always had my back. Thank you is too small of a word.

Thank you to my rock, the love of my life, my husband, Shawn. You are my happily ever after, the man I've been waiting for, the one who helped me change all my narratives. Thank you for your love, for reading all my crummy first drafts, for laughing at my lame jokes, and for always seeing the best in me, even when I can't. I love you bigger than the stars.

To my Creator…thank you is my constant prayer to you. I do not deserve this beautiful life, but you've blessed me anyway. Thank you.

Hope series

Learn more about the Hope series at
crissilangwell.com/hope-series.

Crissi's Books

Fiction

The Road to Hope (Hope series, Book 1)

Jill Johnson loses her toddler son to an unexpected accident. Maddie Russo is a teen mother on the run, rejected by her parents and left on her own. Both have been handed a life neither was prepared for. But through one shared moment in time, they're about to change the other's life. *The Road to Hope* shares a story of overcoming tragedy and making things new from the pieces of broken lives.

Hope at the Crossroads (Hope series, Book 2)

No longer homeless, Maddie is ready for a promising future. Her new family loves and supports her as a single mother, college is on the horizon, and with a brand new relationship, this summer is sure to be the start of something wonderful. But when a face from her past comes back into her life, Maddie has some decisions to make—and her choice will change everything.

Loving the Wind: The Story of Tiger Lily and Peter Pan

See Neverland through the eyes of Tiger Lily, princess of the Miakoda Tribe. Her people share legends of the boy who flies like the birds, lives with the fairies, and harbors a stolen moon, but Tiger Lily doesn't believe the stories until she meets Peter Pan aboard Captain Hook's ship. Worse, the flying thief seems to have stolen her heart.

Come Here, Cupcake (Dessert for Dinner series, Book 1)

Morgan Truly never wanted to come home to Bodega Bay. But when her mother takes a turn for the worse, Morgan packs up her life in Seattle and heads back to her sleepy coastal hometown, taking on a job at the local dessert shop. She soon learns there are perks to being home. First, there's that rugged sailor who can't seem to get enough of her sweets. And second, no one else can either—because who can resist enchanted desserts? Morgan discovers she has magical abilities that involve her baking. Unfortunately, her magic is the very thing that could take her happiness away.

A Symphony of Cicadas (Forever After series, Book 1)

Cast into the afterlife, Rachel Ashby helplessly witnesses the remnants of the life she left behind and the undoing of her fiancé after her death. The longer she remains close, the more he falls apart. Rachel must make a choice—stay near the man she loves, or let go and move beyond.

Forever Thirteen (Forever After series, Book 2)

Joey Ashby died with his mother in a car accident when he was only thirteen. Being stuck forever at such an awkward age is bad enough. But when he sees the trauma his bullied best friend is facing in the world of the living, he knows he needs to step in. However, there's only so much a spirit in the afterlife can do.

Non-Fiction

Reclaim Your Creative Soul

If you're a writer, artist, or musician with a full-time job or young family, you know how hard it is to find time for the creative side of your life. Through tips on organizing your space, budgeting your money, getting in touch with your spiritual side, and more, this book promises to help you find time for your craft—even if you can't quit your day job.

See all of Crissi Langwell's books at crissilangwell.com

About the Author

Crissi Langwell lives in Petaluma, California, and is the author of 10 books. Her main genre is contemporary fiction geared toward women, and she loves writing fiction and non-fiction books that inspire people to do great things. Crissi is a wife, mother, stepmother, dog lover, and wannabe hermit. Her idea of a perfect Friday evening is snuggled up in bed with a good book.

crissilangwell.com